Robert Cartwright

Shakspere and Jonson

Dramatic, versus wit-combats. Auxiliary forces: Beaumont and Fletcher,

Marston, Decker, Chapman, and Webster

Robert Cartwright

Shakspere and Jonson
Dramatic, versus wit-combats. Auxiliary forces: Beaumont and Fletcher, Marston,
Decker, Chapman, and Webster

ISBN/EAN: 9783337394165

Printed in Europe, USA, Canada, Australia, Japan

Cover: Foto ©Andreas Hilbeck / pixelio.de

More available books at **www.hansebooks.com**

SHAKSPERE AND JONSON.

DRAMATIC, *versus* WIT-COMBATS.

AUXILIARY FORCES:—

BEAUMONT AND FLETCHER, MARSTON, DECKER,

CHAPMAN, AND WEBSTER.

LONDON:

JOHN RUSSELL SMITH,

36, SOHO SQUARE.

———

" TWELFTH NIGHT," 1864.

———

Price Four Shillings.

SHAKSPERE AND JONSON.

Of the two following extracts from *Lady Morgan's Memoirs*, the first is singularly applicable to Jonson, and the second to Shakspere :—

> " One almost wonders that some of the fine ladies whom Lady Morgan produced in her works, etching them in aquafortis and colouring them to the life, did not assassinate her by way of return, especially as she invariably introduced a sketch of herself in one corner of all her pictures, taking up all the wisdom and common sense going, as well as being the most agreeable character in the story."—Vol. ii., p. 33.

> " The history of this curious friendship is detailed in the story of the *Wild Irish Girl*, where her father figures as the Prince of Innismore, Mr. Everard and his son as Lord M— and Mortimer; though the beautiful atmosphere of romance which clothes the story in the novel, was entirely absent in the matter of fact."—Vol. i., p. 277.

By the early commentators Jonson was, " for the most part, jeered at or condemned, as a boastful and malignant man, in the world of letters; and as a tetchy, quarrelsome, ungrateful, and ill-conditioned person, in all that related to social life." But Gifford says, " that Jonson, far from being vindictive, was one of the most placable of mankind : he blustered, indeed, and talked angrily; but his heart was turned to affection, and his enmities appear to have been short-lived, while his friendships were durable and sincere."

B

Without entering into the inquiry how far Gifford may have vindicated Jonson from the charges of Steevens and Malone, it will be clearly demonstrated in the following pages, there must have been at one time a violent quarrel between the two poets; that it was sought for by Jonson, unprovoked; and although Shakspere after each encounter entreats for peace, yet the other will ha' none on it, feeling his forces renewed, Antœus-like, by each fall, and from the same source, mother earth.

The battle commenced, or rather the first signs or prognostications of a possible storm appeared in 1596, with the prologue to *Every Man in his Humour*, in which Jonson comes forward as a dramatic reformer; and though the lines may by some be regarded as merely expressing the zeal and earnestness of the author, they can scarcely be regarded as written in a friendly spirit.

The comedy was brought out at the *Globe* in 1598, and "this arose, as some authors assert, from generosity on Shakspere's part;" whilst Gifford asserts, that " his merits must be confined to procuring for his own theatre an improved copy of a popular performance."

Jonson then brings forth one play annually; *Every Man out of his Humour* in 1599, *Cynthia's Revels* in 1600, and *The Poetaster* in 1601.

In *Cynthia's Revels*, Jonson, it is supposed, intended " to ridicule the quaint absurdities of the courtiers;" but as " Marston and Decker were the most conspicuous amongst these dissentients," it must be presumed, that under the name of *courtiers* was concealed an attack on the follies of the poets; and the following passage appears decisive of the author's intention, where he himself, as Crites, passes sentence on the *courtiers*:—

> " And after penance thus performed you pass
> In like set order, not as Midas did,
> To wash his gold off into Tagus' stream;
> But to the well of knowledge, Helicon ;
> Where, purged of your present maladies,
> Which are not few, nor slender, you become
> Such as you fain would seem, and then return,
> Offering your service to great Cynthia."—Act v., sc. 3.

these lines must surely refer to poets.

The only characters applicable to Marston and Decker are Hedon and Anaides; who then are Amorphus the deformed, and Asotus the prodigal? they are not only the two leading characters, but they are, in a manner, separated from the other courtiers, and brought more immediately into contact with Crites; they are thus described in the Induction:—"These, in the court, meet with Amorphus, or the deformed, a traveller that hath drunk of the fountain, and there tells the wonders of the water. With this Amorphus there comes along a citizen's heir, Asotus, or the Prodigal, who, in imitation of the traveller, who hath the Whetstone following him, entertains the Beggar, to be his attendant."

Here we have Amorphus, the deformed, a name highly appropriate to Euphues or Lyly, with his page Cos, the Whetstone, reminding us of Eumenides with his love " Semele, the very wasp of all women;" and although painted in the ridiculous character of Master of the Ceremonies, again extremely apposite, he is in fact, a satirist throughout, and incidentally of the very

follies he affects. The name of Asotus, or the Prodigal,
is also peculiarly appropriate to Shakspere, who " con-
centrates every excellence in his own person,—casting
out, with the profusion of a superior spirit, intellectual
wealth of all kinds upon us;" but probably it was envy
of his wealth that gave the name; and this opinion is
justified by Cupid's account of the lady Argurion or
money, " she loves a player well and a lawyer infinitely;
but your fool above all." Like Amorphus he has a
page, Prosaites or the Beggar, and is afterwards favoured
with an additional one, the Fool.

In the Induction we also read:—" O, [I had almost
forgot it too,] they say, the *umbræ* or ghosts of some
three or four plays departed a dozen years since, have
been seen walking on your stage here; take heed, boy,
if your house be haunted with such hobgoblins, 'twill
fright away all your spectators quickly." This caustic
observation can refer only to Shakspere's plays; as
Love's Labour's Lost was published in 1598, *Romeo and
Juliet* in 1599, *Midsummer Night's Dream* in 1600, and
probably *All's Well that Ends Well* was re-written about
the same time, and very likely *Pericles* and *The Merry
Wives of Windsor.*

The remark of Crites, that Asotus is " no bred-
courtling," applies most appositely to Shakspere's want
of an University education; and by his addressing the
ladies in the words of Amorphus, he becomes " a crow
beautified with our feathers," and Crites calls him " a
jack-daw;" he is also styled Polyphragmon, one that
can do every thing, or " in his own conceit the only
Shakescene in a country;" and his saying, " Nay, sir,

I have read history," must be an allusion to the "York and Lancaster long jars." We are reminded of sweet bully Bottom, and of Sir John Falstaff in *The Merry Wives of Windsor*, when Mercury says:—" I wonder this gentleman should affect to keep a fool: me-thinks he makes sport enough with himself;"—and " a quick nimble memory " recalls to us Sir Hugh's opinion of William, " he is a good sprag memory ;" whilst "*victus, victa, victum*," is redolent of " *hic, hæc, hoc ;*" and " feign to have seen him in Venice or Padua " explains itself.

It is said of the liquid tests of arsenic, that each, singly, is of little value, but, taken all together, they are proof, the substance must be arsenic ; and so it may be said of the numerous traits of character in Asotus : each, singly, may be applicable to any individual, but all apply to Shakspere, and *to him alone are they all applicable;* consequently, Asotus must be Shakspere, whilst Amorphus, the deformed, with his page Cos and his Pythagorical breeches, is and can be no other than John Lyly. We thus see, that in *Cynthia's Revels* Jonson's real object was to make Shakspere and Lyly ridiculous [as well as Marston and Decker] under pretence of ridiculing the quaint absurdities of the courtiers.

The *Poetaster* was brought out at the *Blackfriars* by the children of the Queen's Chapel in 1601. In this drama Marston and Decker are satirised under the names of Crispinus and Demetrius ; and in the character of Ovid, Jonson rejects Shakspere as a dramatist.

The play opens with Ovid in his study, making verses, "songs and sonnets," to the neglect of the law, and in this first scene the allusions to Shakspere are numerous,

clear, and pointed; a law-student, his writings full of
law terms; his descent and name; never blotted a line,
"the hasty errors of our morning muse;" a playmaker
and a stager; and the observation of Tucca, " my noble
neophyte, my little grammaticaster," directly connects
Ovid with Asotus; and "my pretty Alcibiades " is an
allusion to *Timon of Athens.*

With regard to the expression, "*your songs and
sonnets,*" it should not be overlooked, that Meres says,
"As the soul of Euphorbus was thought to live in
Pythagoras, so the sweet soul of Ovid lives in mellifluous
and honey-tongued Shakspere.   Witness his *Venus and
Adonis,* his *Lucrece,* his sugred sonnets among his
private friends."

That there may be no mistake, that Ovid is and shall
be Shakspere, the whole of the last scene in the fourth
act is a parody on the third and fifth scenes in the third
act of *Romeo and Juliet.*

In the scene where the poets personate the gods,
Ovid represents Jupiter; the whole is a parody of the
latter part of the first book of the *Iliad,* which very book
Shakspere had freely paraphrased in the opening of
Henry VI.   Here we have Shakspere as Jupiter, the
great dramatist and theatrical manager as bully Bottom,
or the only Shakescene in his own conceit; but he is
only the mock Jupiter of a false poetical hierarchy, a
set of "*counterfeits,*" and he is dismissed in disgrace as
unworthy of the classical court of Cæsar; and whilst
Shakspere, as Ovid, is summarily dismissed, Chapman,
as Virgil, is enthroned with the following adulatory
strain :—

Cæs. "See, here comes Virgil; we will rise and greet him.
Welcome to Cæsar, Virgil, &c.
Where are thy famous Œneids? do us grace
To let us see and surfeit on their sight."

That Virgil is Chapman may be gathered from the
words of Cæsar :—

"Now he is come out of Campania,
    I doubt not he hath finish'd all his Œneids."

Chapman had probably finished his translation of the
Iliad at this time, although it was not published till
after the accession of King James. He was also Jonson's
most intimate friend, who told Drummond, "he loved
Chapman." Nor can we doubt, Propertius is Dr. Donne,
whom Jonson "esteemed the first poet in the world for
some things." Chapman took the earliest opportunity
of repaying Jonson for his enthronement, by commendatory verses on Sejanus, too fulsome even for Gifford.
Assuredly Shakspere, though a crow and a jack-daw,
showed his good sense in abstaining from such poetical
cawing.

From this analysis of the *Poetaster*, it must be
granted, the Ovid of Jonson, like the Ovid of Meres,
is Shakspere.

When we look to Shakspere's antecedents, to *Parolles*,
Pistol, and *Love's Labour's Lost*, we feel confident, such
a "*crack*" would not tamely submit to these imper-
tinences and insults, especially from such an original, a
very godsend to a satirical joker; can it then be doubted,
that in *Timon of Athens*, a play containing a prodigal
beggar'd and a snarler, Shakspere pours forth his wrath
on Jonson as Apemantus, the churlish philosopher, and

repays the Ovidean compliment by cudgelling the crab-
stick with pitiless contempt and ridicule as Thersites, in
Troilus and Cressida?

In such profound archœological researches dates are
of singular value, and in *Jack Drum's Entertainment,*
1601, is this passage :—

> " Come, I'll be as sociable as Timon of Athens ; "

however slight this evidence of the date of *Timon* may
appear, let it not be forgotten, Mr. Armitage Brown
fixed the very early date of *Hamlet,* contrary to received
opinions, on still slighter grounds.   But there is also
strong internal evidence to the same effect—*Hamlet* was
certainly amended and enlarged in 1600 or 1601 ; and
numerous phrases in *Timon,* even whole passages, remind
us of *Hamlet,* as the quibbling on the words *honest* and
lie ; thus Timon's welcome to Alcibiades :—

Tim.   " 'Ere we depart, we'll share a bounteous time
          In different pleasures."
Ham.   " We'll teach you to drink deep, ere you depart."

Flav.   " I must be *round* with him."
Pol.   " No, I went *round* to work.
          Let her be *round* with him."

Flav.   " What shall defend the *interim ?* "
Ham.   " It will be short : the *interim* is mine."

Tim.   " With thy most *operant* poison."
P.King. " My *operant* powers."

Tim.   " There's ne'er a one of you but trusts a knave,
          That mightily deceives you."
Ham.   " There's ne'er a villain, dwelling in all Denmark,
          But he's an arrant knave."

It should be mentioned, the words *round, interim,* and *operant,* or at least those expressions, are not in the first sketch of *Hamlet.*

As *Timon* was most probably an instant reply to the *Revels,* written at fever-heat without correcting "the hasty errors of our morning muse," it may be surmised *Hamlet* was more leisurely re-written after *Timon,* and this circumstance may account for the "thoughtful philosophy" in the amended play; consequently several sharp sentences, not in the first sketch, are in reality gentle hints or lashes at Jonson; and consequently the passage about an aiery of children, so fully elaborated in the amended copy, deserves consideration; and it may be conjectured, that Shakspere, though he had not altogether retired from London, was at least occasionally a resident at Stratford; the phrase "Hercules and his load," may be a rap at the bricklayer and his hod :—

Ham.   "Do they hold the same estimation they did when I was in the city?   Are they so followed?"
        "Do the boys carry it away?
Ros.   Ay, that they do, my lord; Hercules and his load too.
Ham.   It is not very strange: for my uncle is king of Denmark.
        'Sblood, there is something in this more than natural, if philosophy could find it out."

That the *Poetaster* was written after the amended *Hamlet* may be inferred from the following extracts; such resemblances could not be accidental :—

"Are there no players here? no poet apes,*
That come with basilisk's eyes, whose forked tongues
Are steep'd in venom, as their hearts in gall?

---

* *Vid.,* Epigram, 56, on Poet-Ape, written very likely about this period.

Here, take my snakes among you, come and eat,
And while the squeez'd juice flows in your black jaws,
Help me to damn the author."
" Of base detractors and illiterate apes."

Prologue to the Poetaster.

Ham. " Like the famous ape," &c.
     " There's letters seal'd: and my two school-fellows,—
     Whom I will trust, as I will adders fang'd,—"
Ros. " Take you me for a sponge my lord ? "
Ham. " Ay, sir, that soaks up the king's countenance, his
rewards, his authorities. But such officers do the king
best service in the end : He keeps them, like an ape, in the
corner of his jaw; first mouthed, to be last swallowed ; when
he needs what you have gleaned, it is but squeezing you, and
sponge, you shall be dry again."—*Hamlet.*

There is, however, additional and very singular evidence, not only that *Timon* was written about this
period, but that both it and *Cynthia's Revels* are
founded on the same piece, on another *Timon,* which
has been edited by Mr. Dyce, for the " Shakspere
Society."

With our present knowledge there cannot be the
slightest doubt, Shakspere, as well as Jonson, was
favoured with a copy of it ; and on examination we
shall find, Jonson has drawn far more largely upon it in
Cynthia's Revels than Shakspere did.

Pseudocheus, *a lying traveller,* and Gelasimus, *a city
heir,* in love with the daughter of Philargurus, are not
so much the prototypes as the identical characters,
Amorphus, *the traveller,* and Asotus *a citizen's heir,* son
to the late deceased Philargyrus, and in love with Lady
Argurion ; and Blatte, the prattling nurse, is the same
as mother Moria, or mistress Folly.

The scene between Amorphus and Asotus in Act i., scene 1, may be regarded as a transcript of the following passage :—

Pseud. "A spruce neat youth: what if I affront (accost) him?
Gelas. Good gods, how earnestly do I desire
His fellowship ! was I ere so shamefac'd ?
· What if I send and give to him my cloak?
Pseud. What shall I say? I saw his face at Thebes
Or Sicily? [*aside.*
Gelas. I'll send it. Pœdio,
Give him this cloak ; salute him in my name ;
H'st, thou may'st tell him, if thou wilt, how rich
My father was. [*aside to Pœdio.*
Pseud. What, as a token of his love, say'st thou?
Return this answer to that noble youth ;
I, Pseudocheus from the Bloody Tower,
Do wish him more than twenty thousand healths;
Who 'ere he be, be he more fortunate
Than they that live in the Isles Fortunate,
Or in the flourishing Elizian fields ;
May he drink nectar, eat ambrosia !
Gelas. How daintily his speech flows from him !
Lord, what a potent friend have I obtained !—
What countryman I pray you, sir? "
Act i., scene 4.

Pseudocheus and Gelasimus exchange rings just as Amorphus and Asotus do beavers; the wooing scene is also similar; and we have the word *whetstone,* "wine is valour's whetstone."

Furthermore we have in this "academic Timon" the names of Demetrius and Albius; whilst Hermogenes and Callimela are the same individuals as Hermogenes and Chloe in the *Poetaster.*

The line " and now live like camelions by th' air,"

probably gave rise to the quibble in the amended *Hamlet* :—

> *King.* " How fares our cousin Hamlet ?
> *Ham.* Excellent, i' faith; of the camelion's dish : I eat the air, promise-crammed : you cannot feed capons so."

From this analysis of the drama we are led to presume the author was " a young gentleman of the two Universities," a friend of Jonson's, and well read in Lyly, whom he ridicules as Pseudocheus, whilst the ignorant and unclassical Shakspere is Gelasimus, who has a fall from Pegasus, and is capped with the ears of an ass. Timon may be the author himself, and Laches, *the honest steward,* Jonson ; possibly the two lying philosophers are Marston and Decker.

There is something peculiar about the history of *Troilus and Cressida,* it was published piratically in 1609, and described as " a new play, never stal'd with the stage ;" it was, however, written at this period, and no doubt, in circulation amongst private friends, to-wit the " Mermaid Club." In the prologue we read :—

> " And hither am I come
> A prologue arm'd,—but not in confidence
> Of author's pen or actor's voice ;"

and in the prologue to the *Poetaster* :—

> " *Enter* Prologue *hastily in armour.*"
> " If any muse why I salute the stage
> An armed Prologue ;—
> Whereof the allegory and hid sense
> Is, that a well erected confidence
> Can fright their pride, and laugh their folly hence."

Surely the one is an allusion to the other, and it should

be noted, these are the only instances in which either author has a prologue armed.

If Dr. Johnson objects to Neoptolemus as a name for Achilles in *Troilus and Cressida*, Shakspere may reply that Ben Jonson had previously used it in the *Poetaster* :—

> *Tuc.* "Give me thy hand, Agamemnon; we hear abroad thou art the Hector of citizens : What say'st thou? are we welcome to thee, noble Neoptolemus ? "

We thus have a remarkably strong link connecting these two plays, and the observation of Thersites, " Now she sharpens ;—Well said, whetstone," shows Shakspere had not quite forgotten *Cynthia's Revels*.

Let us examine these four plays in the reverse order, confining ourselves in the strictest manner to the barest evidence the plays afford. In *Troilus and Cressida* the character of Thersites, be it accidental or intentional, is an inimitable caricature of Crites and Horace, that is, of Jonson. In 1601 appeared the *Poetaster ;* in it Ovid is a law student, writing " songs and sonnets ;" he is spoken of as a playmaker and a stager, and acknowledges he has " begun a *poem* of that nature ;" he is in love with Julia, and one whole scene is a parody on *Romeo and Juliet*, at that very time Shakspere was in literary circles called Ovid, on account of his "sugred sonnets ;" can it then be denied, can it for a moment be doubted, that Ovid in the *Poetaster* is intended for Shakspere? In this comedy the witty and accomplished Horace is pestered and bored by a *poetaster*, and escapes from him on the arrival of two other persons ;—in *Troilus and Cressida*, Thersites makes his appearance *in a*

similar manner, being belaboured by the beef-witted
Ajax, and makes his escape on the arrival of Achilles
and Patroclus; and throughout the play his conduct
and remarks are a parody on Horace; Thersites must
consequently be an intentional caricature of Jonson.

In 1600 the *Comical Satire*, or *Cynthia's Revels*,
was acted by the children of the Queen's Chapel;
Asotus the prodigal, with his two pages, the beggar and
the fool, has many traits of character applicable to
Shakspere, and to no other individual;—*Timon of
Athens* contains a prodigal beggar'd, and a churlish
philosopher; both plays are founded on the "academic
Timon;" the date of *Timon of Athens* is unknown, but
the name was familiar to a London audience in 1601,
the play contains also internal evidence, it must have
been written immediately before or after the amended
Hamlet : as Thersites has been shown to be a rejoinder
to Ovid, the natural inference is, that Apemantus is the
reply to Asotus. We may then place these plays in
the following order :—

Cynthia's Revels, in the Summer,	} 1600.
Timon of Athens, in the Autumn,	
Poetaster, in the Summer,	} 1601.
Troilus and Cressida, in the Autumn,	

Many a man has been hanged on circumstantial
evidence far less clear and absolute than these dates,
consequently Apemantus and Thersites must be the
rebound, the repercussive blows to Asotus and Ovid.
Shakspere evidently enjoys Thersites as an intellectual
exercise, " a wit-combat :"—

Hect. "What art thou, Greek, art thou for Hector's match? Art thou of blood and honour?

Thers. No, no;—I am a rascal, a scurvy railing knave, a very filthy rogue.

Hect. I do believe thee ;—live." [*exit.*

That Shakspere felt he was doing battle for Lyly as well as for himself, appears from the following passage, reminding us of Midas, and concisely describing Jonson as a compound of wit and malice :—

> *Ther.* "To what form, but that he is, should wit larded with malice, and malice farced with wit, turn him to? To an ass were nothing, he is both ass and ox; to an ox were nothing, he is both ox and ass."

As evil deeds bear the seeds of their own punishment, it may be conjectured, that the scene from *Homer*, where Ovid acts Jupiter, gave Shakspere the idea of lampooning Jonson as Thersites, just as the playing on the word Judas may have reminded Lyly of Midas.

As the two comedies, *Cynthia's Revels* and the *Poetaster*, were acted by the children of the Queen's Chapel, and the two preceding ones by Shakspere's company, it may be reasonably presumed, some misunderstanding had intervened ; but on examining *Every Man out of his Humour*, to our astonishment, we find the same characters and the same satire as in *Cynthia's Revels ;* but though Shakspere took a part in *Every Man in his Humour*, he did not act in the other, as Gifford innocently observes :—"This comedy, like the former, appears to have been acted by the whole strength of the house, with the exception of Shakspere, who found perhaps no part in it suited to his gentle conditions."

Let us now take a look at the characters in *Every Man out of his Humour* :—Puntarvolo (Lyly) is a copy of Sir Tophas and Don Armado, or rather he is Count Lafeu in their clothes; at his first appearance his *gracing* is a paraphrase of Sir Tophas in *Endymion*, Act ii. sc. 2; and his ready insight into the character of Shift reminds us of Lafeu and Parolles; " he was first smoked by the old lord Lafeu." His *character*, the description of Armado, as well as Mercury's account of Amorphus, are too similar to be accidental. He is spoken of as having a " good knotty wit,"—as " that stiff-necked gentleman,"—" a good tough gentleman, he looks like a shield of brawn at Shrove-tide, out of date, and ready to take his leave." His treatment of Carlo Buffone at the *Mitre*, " I shall be sudden I tell you," raises a suspicion, that Justice Clement in *Every Man in his Humour* is another satirical picture of John Lyly, especially as Daniel is satirised in that as well as in this comedy.

Fungoso (Shakspere), is kinsman to Justice Silence and godson to Puntarvolo, a lawyer's clerk, the son of a yeoman, though a gentleman himself; a rook, a painted jay; he and Asotus are birds of a feather, the self-same individual; and in *Cynthia's Revels* Hedon speaks of Asotus as :—" some idle Fungoso, that hath got above the cupboard since yesterday." Act. iv. sc. 1.

Carlo Buffone, " *thou* Grand Scourge," is of course Marston, the author of the *Scourge of Villianie.*

Fastidious Brisk is consequently Decker.

Shift is Captain Bobadil tamed down and put to his shifts.

Deliro and Fallace are the same individuals as Albius and Chloe in the *Poetaster*.

Asper or Macilente is Jonson " with his wild quickset beard."

The rustics cutting down Sordido after hanging himself, is paraphrased from the clowns in *Hamlet*, and *Plowden's Report* had been previously alluded to amongst the law-books. Certain characters then run through these three comedies, and may be thus arranged :—

Every Man out of his Humour.	*Cynthia's Revels.*	*Poetaster.*
Puntarvolo.	Amorphus.	———
Fungoso.	Asotus.	Ovid.
Carlo Buffone.	Hedon.	Crispinus.
Fastidious Brisk.	Anaides.	Demetrius.
Deliro.	Citizen.	Albius.
Fallace.	His wife.	Chloe.

The characters of Sordido, Fungoso, and Fallace, and Fido, like Obba, strewing flowers on the ground, as well as the words, *macilente*, and the *Isles Fortunate*, leave no doubt Jonson had seen the *Academic Timon* before he wrote *Every Man out of his Humour.* The following passage is regarded as a reflection against *Twelfth Night* and the romantic drama : " as of a duke to be in love with a countess, and that countess to be in love with the duke's son, and the son to love the lady's waiting maid ; some such cross wooing."

To this attack Shakspere indignantly replied by painting Jonson as Don John in *Much Ado about Nothing :* Marston and Decker appear as Claudio and Benedick in the opening of the play, and Beatrice's remark, " Is there no young squarer now, that will

make a voyage with him to the devil?" is clearly
an allusion to Fungoso's admiration for Fastidious
Brisk. The following extract is very significant;
Conrade says to Don John :—

> *Con.* "You have of late stood out against your brother,
> and he hath ta'en you newly into his grace; where it is
> impossible you should take true root, but by the fair weather
> that you make yourself; it is needful that you frame the season
> for your own harvest.
>
> *D. John.* I had rather be a canker in a hedge, than a rose
> in his grace; and it better fits my blood to be disdain'd of all,
> than to fashion a carriage to rob love from any; in this, though
> I cannot be said to be a flattering honest man, it must not be
> denied that I am a plain-dealing villain."

and Don John further observes, "that young start-up
(Claudio) hath all the glory of my overthrow; if I can
cross him any way, I bless myself every way." These
words are mild compared with Macilente's hatred of
Carlo. Marston was a prophane jester, and that accounts
for Claudio's observation ;—

> *Claud.* "All, all; moreover, God saw him when he was
> hid in the garden."

The comedy ends just as pointedly as it opened, since
Decker (Benedick) was the one selected to write against
Jonson :—

> *Bene.* "Think not on him till to-morrow; I'll devise thee
> brave punishments for him."

Having given vent to his wrath in *Much Ado about
Nothing*, Shakspere then, filled with those gentle dis-
positions, which Gifford grants him, attempts the
soothing process in the beautiful comedy of *As you like*

it; in which Jonson is pointed at as Oliver, and, we presume, the young Orlando is our gentle Willy.

Jonson was a posthumous son, brought up by his step-father; and the following lines apparently allude to that circumstance; on returning from the wrestling match Orlando is thus addressed by Adam :—

Adam. "O unhappy youth,
Come not within these doors; within this roof
The enemy of all your graces lives :
Your brother—[no, no brother; yet the son—
Yet not the son ;—I will not call him son,—
Of him I was about to call his father."]

The passage describing the repentance of Duke Frederick is probably an allusion to Jonson's conversion to Popery :—

" Where, meeting with an old religious man,
After some question with him, was converted
Both from his enterprize, and from the world,
His crown bequeathing to his banish'd brother."

The circumstance of this comedy being founded on one of Lodge's novels, affords us a beautiful example, not of Shakspere's idleness and carelessness about his plots, but of the kindliness of his disposition; this is clearly shown by the change of names, Saladyne and Rosader into Oliver and Orlando; whether in the novel the scene is placed in the woods of Arden I know not; but it has been pointed out in the *Footsteps of Shakspere*, that Greene's *Orlando Furioso* was a good-humoured satire on Marlowe; in which play we find the woods of Arden, and the hanging of sonnets on the trees, as well as the names of Orlando and Oliver. There can then be no doubt, that in this beautiful comedy, Shakspere's mind is fondly dwelling on old times and friends long since passed away :—

> Dead shepherd! now I find thy saw of might;
> *Who ever lov'd, that lov'd not at first sight?**
>
> Act iii. sc. 5.

After this analysis of *Every Man out of his Humour,* the reader perhaps will not be surprised to find the same characters in *Every Man in his Humour.*

In this comedy, Justice Clement is evidently intended for Lyly; his threatening Cob with imprisonment for speaking against tobacco is enough to convict him: Cob's date of having been his neighbour eighteen years answers exactly to the publication of *Euphues* in 1580 :—

> *Cob.* "O, the justice, the honestest old brave Trojan in London; I do honour the very flea of his dog. A plague on him, though, he put me once in a villainous filthy fear; marry, it vanished away like the smoke of tobacco; but I was smoked soundly first."

the last words remind us again of Lafeu, "he was first smoked by the old lord Lafeu."

That master Stephen, the country gull, is Shakspere, is no less distinctly marked;—he stands much on his gentility and his reasonable good leg; "why you know," says Stephen, "an a man have not skill in the hawking and hunting languages now-a-days, I'll not give a rush for him; they are more studied than the Greek or the Latin." Like Shakspere, Stephen objects to tobacco, "none, I thank you, sir."

Master Mathew, the town gull, is a satire on Daniel,

---

* A quotation from Marlowe's *Hero and Leander.*

clearly shown by the parody on the first stanza of the
Sonnet to Delia, and the offensive remarks accompanying
it, "these paper-pedlars, these ink-dablers;" and
Mathew's observation, "Downright brags, he will give
me the bastinado," is an allusion to Jonson's satirical
remarks.

George Downright, a plain Squire, is of course
Jonson.

As Hermogenes in the *Academic Timon* is afraid
of Laches, just as Master Mathew is of Downright, it
may be presumed, the character was written in ridicule
of Daniel; and we thus arrive at the probability the
play was produced about Christmas, 1598, and partly
founded on *Every Man in his Humour,* since Downright
and the two gulls appear to be the prototypes of Laches,
Hermogenes, and Gelasimus, and however wretched the
composition of this piece may be considered, the author
has certainly shown considerable originality, since Callimela, is the germ of Fallace and Chloe, and Philargurus
of Sordido, whilst Fungoso and Asotus are far more
nearly allied to Gelasimus than to Master Stephen the
country gull.

To this gratuitous and most malicious attack of *Every
Man in his Humour,** Shakspere replied in *Twelfth Night*
by ridiculing Jonson as Sir Andrew Aguecheek :—

---

* This play bears marks of having been founded on the *Merry Wives
of Windsor;* and it follows, Bobadil is another satirical portrait of
Marlowe, whom Jonson must have seen and probably knew; and his
appearance in the following play as Shift, agrees exactly with the account
of Marlowe :—

> "Now strutting in a silken sute,
> Then begging by the way."

Sir And. " I'll stay a month longer, I am a fellow o' the strangest mind i' the world ; I delight in masques and revels sometimes altogether.

Sir To. Art thou good at these kickshaws, knight ?"

Act i. sc. 3.

Sir To. " He is a knight, dubbed with unhacked rapier, and on carpet consideration ; but he is a devil in private brawl ; *souls and bodies hath he divorced three.*"

Act iii. sc. 4.

His love of wine is not forgotten :—

Mar. " They that add moreover, he's drunk nightly in your company."

But we should lamentably mistake the feelings and indignation of Shakspere, at being so grossly played upon, if we limited his revenge to the humourous character of Sir Andrew ; he had a far sharper shaft in his quiver ;—and when Sir Andrew laughs at the ridiculous contortions and grimaces of Malvolio, 'tis Jonson laughing at the image of his own inordinate vanity and presumption.

In this most veracious of histories, this model of biography, there has been no *cooking ;* long, long ago, it was written, " Biron is not the germ of Benedick ; *he* was played upon ; but had any one attempted to play upon Biron they would have caught a Tartar."*

On making a more minute inspection of *Every Man in his Humour,* we find Shakspere is also represented as young Welbred, and Jonson as his friend, Edward Knowell ; who is, as old Knowell [Chapman] says, " almost grown the idolater of this young Welbred." In *Twelfth Night* Shakspere returns the compliment by painting Jonson as Sebastian, and Capt. Antonio would

---

* *Footsteps of Shakspere,* p. 91.

be Chapman. As Sebastian is beloved by Olivia, whilst Shakspere, as the Duke, is rejected by this haughty and reserved beauty, who then can Olivia be, the adored of two poets? her name tells us, she must be the classical muse the olive, the emblem of Minerva and Athens; whilst Viola is the romantic muse, the virgin violet, the primy spring, the Floscula of *Endymion.* By the marriage of Olivia with Sebastian, Shakspere pays a beautiful tribute to Jonson as a classical scholar.

Furthermore, as Jonson appears to have had Ford in view in the character of Kitely, it follows by a very simple process of deductive philosophy, the two Burghers in *The Merry Wives of Windsor* must be Daniel and Drayton, the two sonnet-poets at the Court of Cynthia, and consequently sweet Ann Page is the expression of Shakspere's admiration for Delia; whilst the fat knight's wooing of Mesdames Page and Ford is a humourous allegory of his admiration and rivalry of those two poets.

I take this opportunity of noting, that in the *Comedy of Errors,* the two brothers or twins, Antipholis of Ephesus and of Syracuse, are Shakspere and Greene; Adriana would be Greene's dramatic muse, and the courtezan would represent his novels. It has been shown in the *Footsteps of Shakspere,* that the double strength of Corsites in Lyly's *Endymion,* refers to Greene's two-fold qualification of writing "stories or poetries;" and Shakspere, in the *Comedy of Errors,* seeks to soothe the wounded vanity and jealousy of his friend by representing his own muse as the younger sister of Greene's, and urging him to cease "paltering up something in prose," and to devote his talents to the drama.

Again, in *Romeo and Juliet*, whilst Juliet is the sonnet-muse,* Helena is the dramatic muse; this allegory is repeated in the *Midsummer-Night's Dream;* —the more these allegorical figures are examined into, the more clear, distinct, and visible they become.

Having thus given, in *Twelfth Night*, his *quid pro quo*, Shakspere, in *Henry V.*, offers Jonson the olive-branch of peace, complimenting him in the character of Jamy as a brave captain of great expedition and knowledge in the ancient wars; and in the prologue, giving a courteous reply to the prologue of *Every Man in his Humour;* but Ben, it seems, preferred being "a canker in a hedge to a rose in his grace;" and again in *As You Like it*, Shakspere makes another generous offer of reconciliation, which apparently had no effect on Jonson, for we find him in *Cynthia's Revels* holding up to ridicule both Shakspere and Lyly in a still more marked and offensive manner; consequently, it is not surprising, that after so much and such uncalled-for provocation, Shakspere's forbearance at last gave way.

It has been shown in Shakspere, Sidney, and Essex, and in 'Juliet' Unveiled, that in several of the early plays the figures of certain dramatists and courtiers stand forth more or less prominent, both dramatist and courtier being represented under the same character; and it would appear, these plays have been constructed on the same plan with similar art or artifice. That Shakspere, in *Timon*, points at the Earl of Essex we

---

* *Vide* 'Juliet' Unveiled.—*Notes and Queries*, 3rd S., iv., 181.

cannot doubt, and whilst the old soldier, for whom
Alcibiades is so much interested, would be Sir Roger
Williams, Apemantus may be more covertly pointed at
Bacon, who was at that time exposed to popular odium
as a false friend to the disgraced earl. We may also
feel certain, notwithstanding the intense passion of the
poet, the play was written before the death of Essex,
otherwise Shakspere would scarcely have satirised him
as the general Alcibiades with his two mistresses. It
was the persistent malice of Jonson, the irony more
polished and the sneer more pointed, in *Cynthia's Revels*,
that excited his anger. It may also be suspected, Essex
is pointed at in the " academic Timon," whilst Bacon
may be the orator Demeas, who is saved from being cast
into prison by Timon's generosity.

Again, in *As You Like it*, Essex appears to be pointed
at in the banished Duke, and especially in the melancholy Jaques, a character, be it noted, that was added
by the poet, and which is as strictly applicable to Essex
as Alcibiades in *Timon of Athens*. Frederick, the usurper,
we presume, is Cecil. But as this comedy was founded on
Lodge's novel, we readily recognise Lodge himself in
the banished Duke, and Greene in Frederick, distinctly
marked by Lodge's withdrawal from the stage, and by
Greene's repentance on his death-bed; and it has already
been shown, that in Oliver and Orlando, Shakspere had
in his remembrance Greene and Marlowe; hence it
follows, in Celia and Rosalind we have a repetition of
the beautiful allegory of Olivia and Viola, as the classical
and the romantic muse; and Shakspere has prettily
changed the name of Alinda in the novel, into Celia or

the *celestial*, whilst Rosalind was not only Lodge's own muse, but also of Spenser, the bard of romance.   However fanciful these opinions may appear, I hold them to be true, and have more delight in discovering these *imaginary* diamonds in the gardens of Shakspere, than picking up nuggets of gold in the fields of Australia.

In *Much Ado about Nothing*, it is acknowledged, William Herbert is shadowed in Benedick, and we may suspect, Don Pedro is Sir Walter Ralegh, and Claudio, the Earl of Southampton, who went with Sir Robert Cecil to France in February, 1598, "leaving behind him a very desolate gentlewoman, who hath nearly cried out her fairest eyes.   They were probably married before his departure; but it was said by the gossips, the marriage did not take place till late in the summer." Don John might be Lord Thomas Howard, Viscount Bindon, with whom Sir Walter had a violent quarrel just about this period. *Vide Gentleman's Magazine*, vol. xli., New Series.

Again, in *Twelfth Night*, we feel confident Ralegh is the Duke, as may be gathered from the following lines :—

" *Sweet violets*, Love's paradise, that spread
   Your gracious *odours*, which yon couched bear
      Within your paly faces,
   Upon the gentle wing of some calm *breathing wind*,
      That plays amidst the plain,
   If by the favour of propitious stars you gain
   Such grace as in my lady's bosom place to find,
      Be proud to touch those places ! "

And how natural, from the lips of Sir Walter, is the exclamation :—

" Too old, by heaven ; let still the woman take
An elder than herself ; "--

Act ii., scene 4.

and thus crumbles into dust the foundation-stone of
Shakspere's domestic unhappiness.

It has been said, there is a statue in every block of
marble; and Shakspere seems to have regarded any
remarkable character, warrior, or statesman, as a man-
mountain, out of which might be struck so many living
figures; Essex to him was such a mass; and although
it may be doubted, whether *Timon* was written before
or after the earl's death, yet we know, Hotspur had
played his hour on the stage by Shrewsbury clock
before 1599, yet has he traits in his character singularly
applicable to the later career of Essex; and whilst it
must have been a labour of love to paint Southampton
as Prince Hal and Henry V., we can scarcely doubt,
Sir Robert Cecil is shadowed in that arch political
dissembler, Henry the Fourth; "a prototype of dip-
lomatic cunning," says Gervinus,—" he has rather
wished than ordered Richard's death." It may also be
suspected, the Earl of Suffolk in *Henry VI.* is another
figure struck out of Essex.

However confident the writer may be in the correct-
ness of these views, he does not pretend to press them
on the reader; but as Shakspere undeniably, in his
earlier as well as in these later plays, shadowed certain
dramatists and courtiers in the *dramatis personæ*, it
may be assumed, he pursued a similar course with
regard to the principal characters in the intermediate
plays.

It may be surmised, Jonson also in some degree followed his example, and it is possible, he has satirised Ralegh in Puntarvolo, and William Herbert in Fastidious Brisk.

That there had been about this period a tempestuous quarrel between Shakspere and Jonson, the following extract is of itself sufficient evidence, and fully justifies the explanation that has been given of these plays. In the *Return from Parnassus*, 1602, Kempe says to Burbage:—" Few of the University pen play well; they smell too much of that writer, Ovid, and that writer, *Metamorphosis*, and talk too much of Proserpine and Jupiter. Why, here's our fellow Shakspere puts them all down: ay, and Ben Jonson too. O that Ben Jonson i a pestilent fellow, he brought up Horace giving the poets a pill; but our fellow Shakspere hath given him a purge that made him bewray his credit."

Furthermore, it appears, that Jonson received from Henslowe, "the 22 June, 1602, in earnest of a book called *Richard Crook-back*, and for new adycions for *Jeronymo*, the sum of x lb."—" From the sum advanced on this play," says Gifford, " the managers must have thought well of it. It has perished, like most of the pieces brought out at their theatre, because they endeavoured to keep them in their own hands as long as possible."

But 'tis a pity *Richard Crookback* has not been preserved, we might then have compared him with Iago, for who can doubt, that Iago is "malignant Ben." The following extracts speak for themselves :—

Rod.   " Thou told'st me, thou didst hold him in thy hate.

Iago.   Despise me, if I do not. Three great ones of
    the city,
    In personal suit to make me his lieutenant,
    Oft capp'd to him :—and, by the faith of man,
    I know my price, I'm worth no worse a place."

    " O villainous! I have looked upon the world for
    four times seven years."

    " The Moor is of a free and open nature,
    That thinks men honest, that but seem to be so;
    And will as tenderly be led by the nose,
    As asses are."

Cass.   " He (Iago) speaks home, madam; you may relish
    him more in the soldier than in the scholar."

Iago is here identified with Macilente:—

Car.   " O, he's a black fellow, take heed of him.
Sog.   Is he a scholar or a soldier?
Car.   Both, both."—
    Every Man out of his Humour, Act i., sc. 1.

Cassio, like Claudio, is Marston; and Montano,
Beatrice's *signior* Montanto, is Decker.

As the exact dates of *Othello* and *Troilus and Cressida*
are not known, and as it is now acknowledged Jonson
was born in 1573, *Othello* may have been, like *Timon*,
written at fever-heat as an instant reply to the *Poetaster ;*
and was followed by *Troilus and Cressida*, just as *Much
Ado About Nothing* was by *As You Like it*, though in a
very different mood. This supposition is confirmed by
the character of the two dramas, the one being all fire
and passion, the other a more elaborate and satirical
composition. As Troilus " ne'er saw three and twenty,"
and as he may be regarded, like Benedick, a compli-

mentary portrait of William Herbert, it may be conjectured, this play was composed in the autumn of 1602;
it also becomes probable, the Earl of Southampton is
intended by Diomedes.

In this "Comical Satire," *Troilus and Cressida*, it
never entered into Shakspere's head nor dawned on his
imagination, to ridicule Homer and the *Iliad*, any more
than I or *Punch*, in our harmless jocularity, might be
guilty of treason to the shades of Hamlet or Othello.
His object in this inimitable parody was to prove his
knowledge of Greek, and take his revenge on Jonson
and Marston; and well has he repaid the former for his
classical attack in the *Poetaster*.

We thus see, that to each of Jonson's attacks Shakspere returns a two-fold blow, at first in a friendly and
courteous spirit, but as the malevolence of the one
increases, so rises the indignation of the other, till at
last "honest, honest Iago" is the expression of Shakspere's scorn and disgust. It may, however, be judged
from the Apologetical Dialogue, that the castigation,
the "putting-down," Jonson had received, was followed
with beneficial results; and as Shakspere played a part
in the tragedy of *Sejanus* in 1603, we may presume, the
two contending poets were reconciled by the interference
of mutual friends. Jonson was at the same time reconciled to Marston and Decker.

We all know, Shakspere knew how to forgive, but
can the same favourable view be taken of Jonson's
conduct; envy and jealousy, so long nourished, are not
so easily rooted out; a personal hostility from his
twenty-second year, apparently causeless, against three

such men as Daniel, Lyly, and Shakspere, is at least a singular circumstance, and it would seem the peace lasted scarcely two years.

In 1605 was brought out *Volpone, or the Fox;* in this comedy Shakspere is ridiculed as Sir Politick Would-be, whilst Jonson appears as Peregrine, a gentleman traveller. I shall make only a few extracts, and refer the reader to the scenes themselves:—" My dearest plots" must mean the historical plays; and " Marry, sir, of a raven that should build in a ship-royal of the king's," is an allusion to Jonson's *Masque of Blackness,* the Queen having a short time before "expressly injoined" the poet to prepare a Masque. Sir Politick's remark, " Alas, sir, I have none, but notes drawn out of play-books," answers for itself. The joke of Sir Politick being concealed under a tortoise-shell, must be a satirical stroke at Caliban, and it would appear, the *Tempest* had been written some months previously, or else corrected and augmented according to Shaksperian usage:—

Per.	" And call you this an ingine?
Sir P.	My own device.
1 *Mer.*	St. Mark! what beast is this?
Per.	It is a fish.
	Farewell most politick tortoise!"—

The Fox, Act v., scene 2.

There cannot be a doubt of Ben's translation into 'Ban, 'Ban, Ca-Caliban. The following extracts evidently allude to Iago and the drunken bricklayer; these passages are probably the retort courteous for some fresh outburst of Jonson's anger at the rejection of *Sejanus:*—

> *Trin.* " By this light, a most perfidious and drunken monster; when his god's asleep, he'll rob his bottle.
>
> *Ste.*   Thou shalt be my lieutenant, monster, or my standard.
>
> *Trin.*   Your lieutenant, if you list; he's no standard.
>
> *Ste.*   ' *Steal by line and level;*' I thank thee for that jest.
>
> *Trin.*   Monster, come, put some *lime* upon your fingers."
>
> —*The Tempest,* Act iv.

From their fondness for finery it is evident, Stephano (Shakspere) is Stephen and Fungoso in *Every Man in* and *out of his Humour,* and Trinculo is Decker.

Shakspere's reply to the *Fox* was that wonderful drama, *King Lear,* in which Jonson is marked out most clearly and unmistakably as Edmund; and it should not be overlooked, the character is an episode, and not in the original history. As Oliver in *As You Like it* can scarcely be called his father's son, is and is not; and as Don John in *Much Ado About Nothing* is the bastard brother of Don Pedro, so Edmund is the bastard brother of Edgar, begot " under the dragon's tail; and my nativity was under *ursa major;* so that it follows I am rough and lecherous ":—

> *Kent.* " Is not this your son, my lord?
>
> *Glo.*   His breeding, sir, hath been at my charge; I have so often blush'd to acknowledge him; that now I am brazed to it."
>
> " He hath been out nine years, and away he shall again."—
>
> *Lear,* Act i., scene 1.

This play is supposed to have been written in the autumn of 1605, and as *Every Man in his Humour* was brought out in November, 1596, consequently "he hath been out nine years."

Nor is it easy to resist the impression, that the following lines have a personal application :—

> *Edg.* " Maugre thy strength, youth, place, and eminence,
> Despite thy victor sword, and fire-new fortune,
> Thy valour and thy heart,—thou art a traitor,
> False to thy gods, thy brother, and thy father."

The allusions to Jonson in this passage are peculiarly apposite, " thy strength, youth, thy victor-sword," and fire-new-fortune, refers to his having written the *Masque of Blackness* by express command of the Queen; whilst "*false to thy gods* " is as good as a date; for only a few months previously, Jonson had made a solemn recantation of his popish errors; unfortunately his heart remained unchanged, a Jesuit still in a Protestant guise.

As Gloster loses his eyes through the treachery of Edmund and by the hand of Cornwall, the latter must be Marston, and Albany, Decker; which opinion is confirmed by the first sentence in the tragedy :—

> *Kent.* " I thought, the king had more affected the Duke of Albany than Cornwall."

The faithful Kent represents Chapman, who was born in 1557, "I have years on my back forty-eight;" and Gloster must be Lyly. This interpretation is again confirmed by the wrangle between Kent, Steward, and Cornwall;—Jonson, as the Steward, is clearly pointed out :—

> *Kent.* " My lord, if you will give me leave, I will tread this unbolted villain into mortar, and daub the wall of a jakes with him."

> " That such a slave as this should wear a sword,
> Who wears no honesty."
> " A plague upon your epileptick visage ! "
> 　　　" None of these rogues and cowards,
> But Ajax is their fool."—
> 　　　　　　　　　　　　　　*Act* ii., scene 2.

The last extract must be a reminiscence of Thersites. Marston is no less distinctly marked by the following imitation of his style :—

Kent.　" Sir, in good sooth, in sincere verity,
　　　　 Under the allowance of your grand aspect,
　　　　 Whose influence, like the wreath of radiant fire
　　　　 On flickering Phœbus' front,—
Corn.　　　　　　　What mean'st by this ?
Kent.　To go out of my dialect, which you discommend so
　much."

Kent being put into the stocks, is of course a satirical allusion to Chapman's imprisonment for ridiculing King James in *Eastward Hoe.*

Let us now take a look at Marston, and see what light he throws on this contest. In the Introduction to his Works, edited by Mr. Halliwell, we read in an extract from Gifford : " the works which our author (Jonson), had chiefly in view, were the *Scourge of Villanie* and the two parts of *Antonio and Mellida.* In the former of these, Jonson is ridiculed under the name of Torquatus, for his affected use of ' new-minted words, such as *real, intrinsicate,* and *delphicke,*' which are all found in his earliest comedies, so that we have here, in fact, little more than the retort courteous."—" It is but fair to add that, whatever Marston might think of the present castigation, he had the good sense to profit by it, since his latter works exhibit but few of the terms here ridiculed."

It is evident Gifford's sagacity is again at fault through his own perversity; as Marston scourged Jonson "for his affected use of new-minted words," it is just possible, the words and phrases, ridiculed in the *Poetaster*, were intentionally coined by Marston in ridicule of Jonson, and on looking into *Antonio and Mellida* such appears to be the fact; for the first part is evidently a burlesque poem or comedy;—Piero is a satire on Jonson; Feliche, a gentle reminiscence of Macilente; and Bobadil and Master Mathew may be the prototypes of Matzagente and Castilio;—in the second or tragical part, Piero becomes a most villainous copy of Claudius, whilst Marston and Shakspere appear as Andrugio and his son Antonio, or the Ghost and Hamlet; Antonio in a fool's habit is the counterpart of Hamlet's feigned madness ; and Maria and Mellida are of course the Queen and Ophelia. This second part, or *Antonio's Revenge,* is undoubtedly founded on the first sketch of *Hamlet,* ed. 1603.—Decker is represented by Alberto, a poor Venetian gentleman, in love with Rosaline, probably a copy of Rosaline in *Love's Labour's Lost.*

The epilogue to the first part being *armed,* very likely gave Jonson the hint of the armed prologue in the *Poetaster;* and he probably also caught the idea of ridiculing *Romeo and Juliet* from the speech at the commencement of the fourth act, where Antonio disguised, escapes from the palace pretending to be in pursuit of Antonio :—

Ant. " Stop, stop Antonio, stay, Antonio.
　　Vain breath, vain breath, Antonio's lost ;
　　He can not find himself, not seize himself,
　　Alas, this that you see is not Antonio,"
　　　　　　　　　　　　　　First Part, Act iv.

The following extracts must be satirical strokes levelled at Jonson, or some other writer :—

Bal. " *Retort and obtuse ;* good words, very good words."
　　" *Respective ;* truly a very pretty word."
　　" *Pathetical and unvulgar ;* words of worth."　　　　.
　　　　　　　　　　　　　　　　Second Part.

Here we are reminded of *Twelfth Night :*—

Sir And. " Good Mistress Mary Accost," &c.
　　" That youth's a rare courtier ! *Rain odours !* well."
　　" *Odours, pregnant,* and *vouchsafed :*—I'll get 'em all
　　　　three ready."

It would thus appear that Jonson very cleverly turned the tables on Marston by pretending to take the new·minted words in *Antonio and Mellida* in a serious light; but though the public may have been gulled by Jonson's ingenuity, the laugh would still be at his expense in literary circles; and in the following year Marston published *Antonio and Mellida.* Even in his ridicule of Shakspere as Asotus, the prodigal with his two pages, the beggar and the fool, Jonson borrows his satire from *Twelfth Night :*—

Sir To. " Why he has three thousand ducats a year.
Mar. Ay, but he'll have but a year in all these ducats; he's a very fool, and a prodigal."

From the following passage we may infer the first part of *Antonio and Mellida* was brought out about Christmas, 1599, and that Marston was born in 1575 :—

Bal. " Lymne them ? a good word, lymne them : whose picture is this? *Anno Domini,* 1599. Believe me, master Anno Domini was of a good settled age when you lymn'd him. 1599 years old ? Let's see the other. *Etatis suæ* 24. Bir Ladie, he is somewhat younger. Belike master ˙Etatis Suæ was Anno Domini's son."—

Act v., scene 1.

The Malcontent.—On comparing the characters in this play with those in *Antonio and Mellida,* we have in the latter, Andrugio, the banished duke of Genoa, with his wife Maria ; and Piero, duke of Venice;—in the *Malcontent,* Altofront (Marston), disguised as Malevole, is the banished duke of Genoa, Pietro (Jonson), is the usurping duke ; Celso, the friend of Altofront, is of course Decker.

In this powerful drama, Marston has given us two vigorously drawn characters ; Malevole is the author himself, and that " huge rascal " Mendoza, might have been a life-like portrait of Shakspere the man himself, had *jaw* predominated over *brow* ; and it may be surmised, we are indebted to this play for the magnificent character of Othello, the grand contrast, the mighty opposite to Mendoza.

Iago's restless jealousy about the Moor's too great familiarity with his wife, has reference to this play,* where Pietro (Jonson), is similarly jealous of Mendoza (Shakspere). This view of the intimate connexion of these two dramas is confirmed by the circumstance, that

---

* The *Malcontent* was probably produced about Christmas, 1600, and transferred a few weeks after, to Burbage and Co., in consequence perhaps of a money-difference with Henslowe.

whilst Iago's wife is named Emilia, and Cassio's mistress, Biancha, the two ladies attendant on the Duchess Aurelia, are also named Emilia and Biancha; such a coincidence can scarcely be accidental. Furthermore, on examining *Troilus and Cressida*, we may reasonably suspect Marston is painted as Pandarus; and at the end of the play Pandarus gives us the plain-spoken language of Marston, and does not hesitate to " nominate a spade a spade." Shakspere was perhaps led to give this character to Marston from Malevole's frequent jests on that subject.

This play, the *Malcontent*, being free from the words ridiculed by Jonson in the *Poetaster*, is strong evidence such new-minted words were used by Marston in *Antonio and Mellida* in a burlesque sense.

The *Dutch Courtezan* probably followed close on the heels of the *Poetaster*, as Marston's retort courteous to that play. Both Shakspere and Jonson are unmistakably ridiculed therein; the one as young Freevill, and the other as Malheureux, *his unhappie friend*; and we may presume the author amuses himself as Cocklcdemoy, a wittie Citie jester. But Shakspere is very gently, even kindly handled in this comedy, and it may, not inaptly, be said, the two poets join in laughing at Jonson as Malheureux, a parody on Crites. Marston is in a very good humour, not at all affected by the emetic pills in the *Poetaster*.

Freevill's expression, "*my dear Lindabrides*," is an allusion to Asotus in *Cynthia's Revels*, Act iii., scene 3; the sweet innocent Beatrice, engaged to be married to Freevill, appears, like Mellida, intended for Ophelia;

this supposition is confirmed by the oft expressed wish of Franciscbina:—

Fra.　　　　　" Freevill is dead, Malheureux sal hang,
And swete divel, dat Beatrice, would but run mad, dat
She would but run mad ; den me would dance and sing."
　　　　　　　　　—Act v., scene 1.

and Beatrice's melancholy observation, " sister, cannot a woman kill herself? is it not lawful to die when we should not live ?" looks like a reminiscence of " Is she to be buried in Christian burial, that wilfully seeks her own salvation ?"

Crispinella, Beatrice's sister, thus describes Freevill,— " But thy match, sister,—by my troth I think 'twill do well; he's a well shapt, cleane-lipp'd gentleman, of a handsome, but not affected fineness, a good faithful eye, and a well-humord cheeke; would he did not stoope in the shoulders for thy sake."—Act iii., scene 1. The nurse thus describes him :—" heers Mistress Beatrice is to be married, with the grace of God ; a fine gentleman he is shall have her, and I warrant a stronge; he has a leg like a post, a nose like a lion, a brow like a bull, and a beard of *most fair expectation ;*" the last phrase reminds us of Asotus' beard, " which is not yet extant ;" and of the words of Petulus in Midas, " my concealed beard."

All, however, ends well; Malheureux is cured of his love, and escapes the gallows for the murder of his friend, by the reappearance of Freevill; whilst Cockledemoy and Mulligrub settle their difficulties to mutual satisfaction.

Eastward Hoe is the joint production of Chapman,

Jonson, and Marston; on examination it falls readily
into three divisions, and there can scarcely be a doubt,
the first act was written by Jonson, the second and
third acts by Marston, and the two last by Chapman.
That the play is an attack on Shakspere is clearly
shown by the ridicule cast on Hamlet and Ophelia in
the third act; and it is equally certain Shakspere is
satirised as the idle apprentice, Francis Quicksilver.

The following lines smack of Shakspere. *Enter*
Quicksilver *drunk :*—

Quick. " Eastward hoe ! Holla, ye pampered ladies of Asia !"
      " Sfoote ! lend me some mony ; hast thou not Hyren
      here ?"
Quick. " When this eternal substance of my soul "—
Touch. " Well said, change your gold ends for your play ends.
Quick. " Did live imprison'd in my wanton flesh "—
Touch. " What then, sir ?"
Quick. " I was a courtier in the Spanish court, and Don
      Andrea was my name."

Act. ii., sc. 1.

The latter lines are evidently a parody on the celebrated passage in *Measure for Measure* :—

      " Ay, but to die, and go we know not where;
      To lie in cold obstruction, &c."

Act. iii., sc. 1.

In the characters of Sir Petronel Flash and his friend
and admirer Quicksilver, we have a repetition of Fasti-
dous Brisk and Fungoso; consequently Sir Petronel
must be Decker; Jonson of course is Goulding, the good
apprentice, and Lyly being depicted as Touchstone adds
greatly to the raciness of this malicious satire.

Although much ink has flowed from able pens, yet the

question remains unsolved, whether *Love's Labour Won,* mentioned by Meres in 1598, was the *Tempest* or *All's Well that Ends Well.* It is easily granted, the comic scenes in the *Tempest* may have been at this time somewhat altered, and pointed at Jonson; but as *Eastward Hoe* appears to be such an unprovoked attack, Shakspere, we may feel confident, would have his revenge, be it wrathful or humourous; and at the very opening of the *Tempest* we find, Prospero has his *three enemies* in his power; consequently if this romantic drama be a reply to *Eastward Hoe,* Prospero must represent Shakspere; —Antonio: Jonson;—Alonso: Chapman;—and Sebastian: Marston;—no other solution of the allegory, no other placing of the characters, can be admitted; and on examination Sebastian is found to be Marston, drawn exactly according to Jonson's account of Carlo Buffone, —"a public, scurrilous, and profane jester, that more swift than Circe, with absurd similes, will transform any person into deformity:"—

> *Seb.* "He receives comfort like cold porridge."
> "Look, he's winding up the watch of his wit;
> By and by it will strike."
> "As if it had lungs and rotten ones."
> Act. ii., sc. 1.

By Alonso's deep grief Shakspere might mean, Chapman regretted or ought to have been ashamed of his conduct.

It has been previously shown, that Stephano and Trinculo are Shakspere and Decker; both of them being drunk, getting wet, and losing their bottles in the pool, and "you'd be king of the isle, sirrah," evidently refers to the ducking Quicksilver and Sir Petronel got in the Thames, in the Pool just below Wapping old stairs; *vide Eastward Hoe*, Act iv., sc. 1

Antonio's remark must be an act of self-recognition :—

> *Ant.* "Very like; one of them
> Is a plain fish, and, no doubt, *marketable*."

Nor has Shakspere forgotten his old friend Lyly, as Gonzalo, the honest old counsellor.

From the intimate connexion between these two plays, so clear and unmistakable, it follows, the *Tempest* must have been originally composed after *Eastward Hoe*, and consequently *All's Well that Ends Well* must be *Love's Labour's Won*.

In the *Tempest*, as in *As you Like it*, Shakspere's mind is again dwelling on olden times; this is made manifest by the remark of Prospero to Ariel :—

> "Imprison'd thou didst painfully remain
> A dozen years."
>
> Act i., sc. 2.

As the *Tempest* was brought out in the spring of 1605, a dozen years carries us back to 1593, when the *Midsummer Night's Dream* was composed, and Jonson commenced his dramatic career. In the conception of Ariel Shakspere evidently had Puck in his recollection; Ariel is Prospero's assistant, and discharges similar offices, just as Puck attends on Oberon; and the expression, "I go, I go," used by both, clearly shows the connexion in the poet's mind. This connexion or resemblance being granted, it follows, Ariel must be another translation, and a divine one into the realms of light, of Nash, who

died about two or three years before the appearance of
the *Tempest*. It is interesting to see, how Shakspere,
to soften the tone of his imbittered feelings in his
quarrels with Jonson, turns his thoughts to his old
friends and foes; the character of Moth and Puck,—of
Iago and Caliban, mark unmistakably the difference of his
feelings towards his two persecutors. Nor did Shakspere
bear any illwill against Marston, in whom there seems
to be something jolly and hearty.

But behind these *dramatic figures,* so visible through
the transparent veil of the *Tempest,* may be seen
another set of figures equally interesting. These
lines :—

> " or that there were such men,
> Whose hands stood in their breasts ? which now we find
> Each putter-out on five for one, will bring us
> Good warrant of,"

have furnished one of the strongest arguments, that the
Tempest must have been written in 1596; but they are
merely a sign-post or door-plate, that Sir Walter
Ralegh is *here* ; we have a similar passage in Othello's
speech, when he gives an account of his wooing of Desdemona :—

> "And of the Cannibals that each other eat,
> The Anthropophagi, and men whose heads
> Do grow beneath their shoulders."

We are justified in believing, this passage also is a sign
or mark of Sir Walter, a diagnostic symptom, literally
" *a mark of wonder* " like the mole or sanguine star on
the neck of Guiderius; it is by these delicate touches or
hints the dates of several plays have been determined.

As Othello's speech is so peculiarly suitable to Sir
Walter, so descriptive of his courtship of Elizabeth,
daughter of Sir Nicholas Throgmorton, there cannot be
a doubt, that in the Moor the romantic dramatist
has given us a portrait of the Elizabethan hero. This
supposition is confirmed by the fact, that Sir Walter
Ralegh was appointed to the government of Jersey
about a year before Othello was appointed governor of
Cyprus; and we may suspect, the " will as tenderly be
led by the nose as asses are " is a gentle reminiscence of
" I should have savoured very much of an ass " in the
Discovery of Guiana. As Bacon appears to be pointed
at in Apemantus, so may Sir Robert Cecil in Iago; and
Roderigo would be Cobham, who was played upon by
Cecil, just as Roderigo is by Iago.

In the *Tempest* the two knights, the heroic Ralegh
and the crafty Cecil, are represented by the two Dukes of
Milan, Prospero and Antonio; King James is Alonso,
King of Naples ; and Sebastian, the sarcastic jester, may
well stand for Sir Edward Coke, the king's attorney;
and Ferdinand * is William Herbert :—

---

* *Ferd.* " Admir'd Miranda—

for several virtues
Have I lik'd several women ; never any
With so full soul, but some defect in her
Did quarrel with the noblest grace she ow'd,
And put it to the foil : But you, O you,
So perfect, and so peerless, are created   ·
Of every creature's best."

Tempest, Act iii., sc. 1.

Bene. " One woman is fair ; yet I am well : another is wise, yet
I am well : another virtuous ; yet I am well ; but till all graces be in
one woman, one woman shall not come in my grace."

Much Ado about Nothing, Act ii., sc. 3.

Pro.   My brother, and thy uncle, call'd Antonio,—
I pray thee, mark me,—that a brother should
Be so perfidious!
                    Of temporal royalties
He thinks me now incapable : confederates
[So dry he was for sway] with the king of Naples,
To give him annual tribute, do him homage;
Subject his coronet to his crown, and bend
The dukedom, yet unbow'd, [alas, poor Milan !]
To most ignoble stooping.
                    Now the condition.
This king of Naples, being an enemy
To me inveterate, hearkens my brother's suit;
Which was, that he in lieu o' the premises,—
Of homage, and I know not how much tribute,—
Should presently extirpate me and mine
Out of the dukedom ; and confer fair Milan
With all the honours, on my brother :" &c.
                                Act i., sc. 2.

Pro.   Most cruelly
Didst thou, Alonso, use me and my daughter;
Thy brother was a furtherer in the act ;—
Thou'rt pinch'd for't now, Sebastian.—Flesh and
   blood,
You brother mine, that entertain'd ambition,
Expell'd remorse and nature."
                                Act v., sc. 1.

As the *Tempest* is a reply to *Eastward Hoe* we may
suspect Sir Petronel Flash is a satire on Sir Walter
Ralegh; his imprisonment, Lady Flash's fruitless
journey eastward after her husband's enchanted castle,
and the name of the play, all have reference to the
Tower. It is gratifying to know, the three malicious
wits met with retributive justice, and were imprisoned
with the pleasant prospect of having their ears and noses

slit more probably on account of the following joke on
his Majesty, than for a satire on the Scots :—

> 1. *Gent.* "On the coast of Dogges, sir; y'are i'th
> Isle of Dogges, I tell you, I see y'ave bin washt in the Thames
> here, and I believe ye were drowned in a tavern before, or else
> you would never have toke boat in such a dawning as this was.
> Farewel, farewel; we will not know you for shaming of you.
> *I ken the man weel; he's one of my thirty pound knights.*"
>
> Act iv., sc. 1.

It seems, however, these three playwrights were also
making themselves merry at the expense of one of King
James' own thirty pound knights, or at least of his lady
in the character of Girtred ; Bacon was desirous of being
knighted, " because I have found out an Alderman's
daughter, a handsome maiden, to my liking." He was
knighted with three hundred others on the 23rd July,
1603, the day of the coronation, and "the handsome and
rich Miss Barnham speedily became Lady Bacon."
*Lives of the Lord Chancellors.**

From the happy termination of each play, it is probable the public did not anticipate for Sir Walter a very

---

* Bacon and his handsome maiden were not married till 1606; and
from the account of Mrs. Barnham in the *Personal History of Bacon*,
it may be inferred, the mother rather than the daughter was the person
ridiculed. It is curious to see, how closely the history of Bacon and
Coke resembles the story of Shakspere and Jonson. The following remarks
remind us of Jonson's satire :—"They had spoken of his vanity, of his
presumption, of his dandyism, of his unsound learning and unsafe law.
—Coke had called him a fool. Cecil had fancied him a dupe." And
so they served Ralegh ; but Shakspere with all his good-nature, gentle-
ness, and poetical temperament, was, as Jonson found to his cost,
neither a fool nor a dupe ; he had the determined will, that Bacon
wanted, and an insight into man, that neither Ralegh nor Bacon had;
and whilst he might have stood for his own Hamlet, Bacon might have
been the Hamlet of Goethe and Coleridge.

prolonged imprisonment, which, however, extended from 1603 to March 1616.

As the *Tempest* is a reply to *Eastward Hoe*, Caliban's rejoicing over his freedom shows it must have been written after the release of the three prisoners; and Ariel's song justifies the inference, it was brought out in May or early in June; nor can there be a doubt, the *Mask of Ceres* was composed in direct competition, as a contrast in its chaste simplicity and classical purity, to Jonson's gorgeous *Masque of Blackness*, which had been performed at Court on the previous Twelfth Night with unusual magnificence. As Jonson prides himself on having written the *Poetaster* in fifteen weeks, we may judge of his intense disgust and rage at being translated into Caliban by his boast of having "fully penn'd" the *Fox* in five weeks.

It has been suggested, that in the line "Freedom, hey-day, hey-day," Shakspere may have had an eye to the song of Prosaites:—

> "Come follow me, &c. hey-day, hey-day;
> And help to bear a part. Hey-day, hey-day."
>
> *Cynthia's Revels*, Act ii., sc. 1.

It is, however, equally probable, Shakspere had also in his recollection the following lines at the end of the tragedy of "*Sejanus; His Fall:*"—

> *Sen.* "And praise to Macro, that hath saved Rome!
> Liberty, liberty, liberty! Lead on,
> And praise to Macro, that hath saved Rome!"

There cannot be a doubt, that in the character of Sejanus, Jonson has satirised Shakspere; Chapman would be Cremutius Cordus, and Jonson, Arruntius and

Macro, and Silius may represent Marston. This thoroughly knavish trick was concocted between Jonson and Marston; whilst Shakspere, so unsuspicious and " as easily led by the nose as an ass," innocently believing in the general pacification, was induced to act a part in the drama. By comparing the characters of Sejanus and Livia with Mendoza and Aurelia in the *Malcontent* we find, Jonson has no less justly than courteously styled his own lines " weaker and no doubt less pleasing " than his coadjutor's in the original play; the speech of Sejanus at the opening of the second scene second act, is probably one of the altered passages. This production being so purely classical and so distinct in its satire from the comedies, may account for Shakspere's Fall into this Confederate trap. On discovering by the jests and inuendos at the *Mermaid* the scurvy trick, the *sell*, for it's worth no other name, that had been played upon him, Shakspere in his wrath hangs up Jonson in a few lines as the drunken Barnardine in *Measure for Measure*, appropriately so named :—

> *Duke.* " What is that Barnardine, who is to be executed this afternoon ?"   .
> *Prov.* " A Bohemian born ; but here nursed up and bred : one that is a prisoner nine years old."
>
> Act iv., sc. 2.

This play must have been, like *Timon*, an instant reply, and was probably produced in the autumn of 1603, just nine years since Jonson's imprisonment in 1594.

Jonson is also severely handled in the character of Angelo. After reading Marston's plays and the poem of *Pygmalion's Image* the reader will readily perceive,

Marston is accurately delineated as the satirical and plain-spoken Lucio; consequently Claudio must be Decker. Shakspere generally speaks through the Duke, in whom appears to be shadowed that easy and familiar monarch, King James; and Escalus is probably intended for Chapman.

Whether the tragedy of *Sophonisba* was written before or after *Macbeth* may be dubious, but we are therein reminded of that drama; it has a ghost, a witch, and at the end a fight between Syphax and Massinissa; a suspicion then arises, *Macbeth* is not quite free from the shadow of Jonson; that the propulsion given to Shakspere's poetic fury by *Volpone* was not exhausted in *Lear*, but flowed over into *Macbeth* :—

> *Oth.* "Like to the Pontick sea,
> Whose icy current and compulsive course
> Ne'er feels retiring ebb, but keeps due on
> To the Propontick and the Hellespont ;
> Even so my bloody thoughts."
>
> *Othello*, Act iii., sc. 3.

and thus it may be presumed, in Macbeth and Macduff we have repeated the hid sense of Edmund and Edgar.

As Jonson peers through the thin guise of Syphax, probably Scipio and Lœlius represent Marston and Decker; and the noble Massinissa must be Shakspere, for whom Marston seems to have the highest esteem and affection; his abuse being more a love of mischief, boisterous fun than ill-will; but, like Shakspere, he generally paints Jonson as envious, malicious, and ungrateful.

Sophonisba was followed apparently by *What you Will*,

D

published in 1607; in this comedy the poet Lampatho
Doria is acknowledged to be the author himself; and with
equal certainty it may be added, Quadratus is Jonson,
and Laverdure, Shakspere, and Faber Simplicius may
be intended for Decker.

Laverdure thus describes himself:—"a straight leg, a
plump thigh, a full vaine, a round cheeke; and, when it
pleaseth the fertility of my chinne to be delivered of a
beard, 'twill not wrong my kissing, for my lippes are
rebels and stand out." It would seem, Shakspere had
a genuine English countenance, a fresh complexion, with
his little trim Elizabethan beard, and was not a hairy
leopard like Greene; whilst "my lippes are rebels"
coincides exactly with Nash's description, "and hang the
lip like a capcase half open," and "a little bit of the
teeth shewing" in the bust at Stratford.

Having reviewed Marston's plays, we can now form
a more correct view of this triple or tripartite contest.
We may take, as a secure basis or ground to build
upon, Jonson's three *Comical Satires*, as he calls them
Every Man out of his Humour was brought out in
1599; *Cynthia's Revels*, in 1600; and the *Poetaster*, in
1601. Shakspere replies to the first in *Much ado about
Nothing*, followed by *As you Like it*; about the same
time, Marston brings out the first and second parts of
Antonio and Mellida; Shakspere then, indignant at
the fresh insults offered to himself and Lyly, in the characters of Amorphus and Asotus, pours forth his wrath
on Jonson as Apemantus, and repays Marston for the
travesty of *Hamlet*, by painting him as the Athenian
general, Alcibiades, a brave soldier but of dissolute

morals. Marston retaliates on Shakspere in the *Malcontent*; and Jonson in the *Poetaster* takes his revenge on both of them. Marston replies again in the *Dutch Courtezan*, and Shakspere repays both Jonson and Marston in *Othello*, as well as in *Troilus and Cressida*.

It may also be conjectured, Marston's attack on *Hamlet* was the immediate cause of its being re-written at this period; Shakspere being, by a singular coincidence, in the same bilious and irritable mood as in 1588, having literally two duels on his hands.

Furthermore, as the amended *Hamlet*, though entered at the Stationers' Company in 1602, was not published till 1604, it becomes highly probable, King James' slight to the memory of Queen Elizabeth, in not allowing any person in black to approach his presence, gave Shakspere the hint for the alteration in the speech of Laertes :—

Laer. "My gracious Lord, your favourable licence,
Now that *the funeral rites* are all performed,
I may have leave to go again to France."

Ed. 1603.

Laer. "Dread my Lord,
Your leave and favour to return to France;
From whence, though willingly, I came to Denmark,
To show my duty in your coronation."

Ed. 1604.

We thus see, Shakspere's knowledge of man was not mere instinct, "but crescent,

as this temple waxes,
The inward service of the mind and soul
Grows wide withall."

Let us now take a look at Decker. In 1601, Jonson

had raised up against himself a host of enemies, law-
yers, soldiers, and players, and Decker had been "put
forward by the rest, and as he was not only a rapid but
a popular writer, the choice of a champion was not
injudicious." Of the *Satiromastix* Gifford says,—"In
transferring the scene from the court of Augustus to
England, Decker has the inconceivable folly to fix on
William Rufus, a rude and ignorant soldier, whom he
terms 'learning's true Mœcenas, poesy's king,' for the
champion of literature, when his brother Henry I. who
aspired to the reputation of a scholar, would have
entered into his plot with equal facility." But William
Rufus, "learning's true Mæcenas, poesy's king," it
may be presumed, was the ignorant William Shakspere,
"skilled in the hawking and hunting languages;" so
that Decker's selection appears to have been peculiarly
appropriate. The wits of Elizabeth were not asleep.

In this comedy, Shakspere is King William, and
Lyly is Sir Vaughan ap Rees; the remark of Tucca,
"be not so tart my precious Metheglin," identifies
Lyly with Amorphus, reminding us of the Metheglin
and Pythagorical breeches in *Cynthia's Revels*, which,
I hold, are satirical allusions to his transmigrations
through Sir Hugh Evans and Captain Fluellen; whilst
in the remark, "you nasty Tortois, you and your itchy
poetry break out like Christmas, but once a year," we
have probably the germ of Caliban.

Northward Ho appears to have been an immediate
reply to *Eastward Hoe;*—Greenshield and Featherstone,
two worthless profligates, are Jonson and Marston;
and Hornet may be intended for Chapman. The

honest citizen Mayberry is Decker, and his friend, the worthy poet Bellamont, is of course Shakspere; and possibly "Have I given it you, master poet? did the limebush take?" may have been the origin of the jesting in the *Tempest* about limetrees, and "I thank thee for that jest, steal by line and level."

The three lovers of Doll, as well as Hornet and his two serving-men, are no doubt intended as additional ridicule of the three authors of *Eastward Hoe*.

Bellamont is a very excellent character, but he has a spendthrift for a son, and pays his debts to release him from prison; this young gentleman, Philip, is also an admirer of Doll, and says to his father,—"You have often told me the nine Muses are all women, and you deal with them: may not I the better be allowed one than you so many." It may then be surmised, Philip is Decker himself, whose life appears to have been a hopeless struggle with poverty; he was frequently confined for debt, and was on one occasion assisted by Alleyn the player. It is probable, he has here gracefully and gratefully acknowledged his obligations to Shakspere.

The satire in this comedy is decidedly against Jonson rather than Marston.

Westward Ho may have been composed about Christmas, 1604; the three citizens, Honeysuckle, Wafer, and Tenterhook, are the three authors of *Eastward Hoe*.

In these two comedies, *Northward Ho* and *Westward Ho*, three is the winning figure. In the one we have the landlord and his two waiters, and Doll's three lovers; in the other, three jealous citizens; and in the

Tempest, Prospero has his three enemies at his mercy; these are three very remarkable coincidences, and capable, apparently, but of one interpretation.

As Chapman was a joint labourer in the production of *Eastward Hoe*, it becomes probable, something may be found in his dramas throwing additional light on this contest, and in *Bussy D'Ambois*, published in 1606, we cannot doubt, that D'Ambois is intended for Jonson, and Monsieur for Marston; this opinion is fully justified by the friendly exchange of personal abuse between Bussy and Monsieur in the third act; the reader will perhaps excuse the insertion of the lines, as they are rather too strong for modern ears. The following passage identifies Jonson with Bussy :—

> *Maff.*   " By your no better outside, I would judge you
>   To be a poet,"—
>   " That is strange,
>   Y'are a poor soldier, are you?
> *Buss.*   I am a scholar, as I am a soldier."
> *Gui.*   " Thou art a bastard to the Cardinal of Ambois."

On finding Kent's abuse of the Steward in *Lear* to correspond so accurately with the language used by Chapman in *Bussy D'Ambois*, it follows, the faithful Kent is a portrait of Chapman, and that *Bussy D'Ambois* preceded *Lear*, which probably was not brought out till Christmas, 1605, as Kent has "years on his back forty-eight." Consequently, Chapman, as well as Marston, must have had a quarrel with Jonson immediately after, or rather before the *Fox;* for it may be suspected, Chapman and Marston are satirised in the characters of Corbaccio and Voltore, whilst Mosca [Jonson] befools

them and vivisects Volpone [Shakspere]. The origin
of the difference may have been Jonson's arrogance
after the success of the *Masque of Blackness*, for D'Ambois is described as capable of any villainy, " do anything
but killing of the king." We do not suppose there
was any personal quarrel on this occasion, merely a
dramatic explosion, and, like enough, the wit-combats
at the *Mermaid* proceeded as usual, only sharpened by
a little tartaric acid to the attic salt. Ben, now finding
the whole court of Cynthia against him, wisely deemed
discretion the better part of valour, and did not continue
the contest, contenting himself with the honours of
being first courtier or Fawne at the court of Phœbus.

On further examination and reflection, we become
more and more assured, *Sophonisba* preceded *Macbeth* ;
that Shakspere was pleased and flattered by being por-
trayed as Massinissa, and repaid Marston by shadowing
him in Banquo. It was the powerful genius, burning
through these two tragedies, the *Malcontent* and *Sophonisba*, that excited Shakspere's emulous admiration, void
of envy.

That there had been a dramatic contest between
Shakspere and Jonson, the writer of these pages cannot
doubt; that there had been at one time a personal
quarrel can scarcely be doubted; and it is certain,
Jonson must have been acquainted with Shakspere,
Lyly, and Daniel before 1598, or even 1596, probably
a frequenter at the *Mitre*, but the good men little knew,
there was a chiel amang 'em takin' notes.

After this fierce struggle, this gladiatorial contest,
there seems to have been peace for several years; but

on looking into the *Silent Woman*, 1609, and the *Alchemist*, 1610, we find undeniable evidence another quarrel had occurred, or at least another dramatic contest is raging.

In the *Silent Woman* Shakspere is ridiculed as Sir John Daw, whose intimate friend, Sir Amorous La Foole, we may suspect, is a caricature of Inigo Jones. Sir John makes his appearance as a Shakescene and a Crow; the following lines are home-thrusts :—

> *Daup.* " Admirable!
> *Clar.* How it chimes, and cries tink in the close, divinely!
> *Daup.* Ay, 'tis Seneca.
> *Clar.* No, I think 'tis Plutarch.
> *Daw.* The dor on Plutarch and Seneca! I hate it: they are mine own imaginations, by that light. I wonder those fellows have such credit with gentlemen.
> *Clar.* They are very grave authors.
> *Daw.* Grave asses! mere essayists: a few loose sentences, and that's all."

The observation about comparing "Daniel with Spenser, Jonson with t'other youth," has been remarked upon as a flirt at Shakspere and a sneer at Daniel, but it is still more remarkable as a specimen of Jonson's vanity. Sir John and Sir Amorous both terminate their career ignominiously, giving up their swords and submitting, the one to so many kicks, and the other to " tweaks by the nose *sans nombre*."

In the *Alchemist* Shakspere appears as Dapper, a greedy and credulous lawyer's clerk, a frequenter of the *Dagger* and the *Woolsack*, two ordinaries or gambling houses of the lowest and most disreputable kind.

Amongst other things, " [*they blind him with a rag*] to show he is fortunate," and the Fairy Queen and fairies pinch him, in allusion to Falstaff.

But Dapper, and Sir Politick in the *Fox*, are merely sign-posts; in these two master-pieces of Jonson, the *Fox* and the *Alchemist*, honest Iago shows he has studied the art of war under his great commander, Othello; Shakspere is aimed at both as Volpone and as Sir Epicure Mammon, and though the one is a gull and the other gulls, yet the basis of each character is the same, lust and covetousness.

As Sir John Daw is spoken of as "living among the wits and braveries too, ay, and being president of them," and Dapper is promised :—

> "those that drink
> To no mouth else, will drink to his, as being
> The goodly president mouth of all the board,"

it may be inferred Shakspere was president of the *Mermaid Club*. In these two comedies, the *Silent Woman* and the *Alchemist*, Jonson appears as Truewit in the one, and Lovewit in the other.

Shakspere's courteous reply to the sneering insults in the *Silent Woman* was that magnificent drama *Coriolanus*, in which Jonson appears as Aufidius, and also as the tribune Sicinius; Shakspere speaks chiefly through Coriolanus :—

> "They have a leader,
> Tullus Aufidius, that will put you to it :
> I sin in envying his nobility :
> he is a lion,
> That I am proud to hunt."—

Act i., scene 1.

As the two tribunes are so similar in character, they may be regarded, and were perhaps intended, for one individual, substance, and shadow;—"thou Triton of the minnows," and "hadst thou foxship to banish him," plainly mark Sicinius as Jonson; to which may be added the words of Aufidius, "five times, Marcius, I have fought with thee;" thus we unmask the intention of the poet, for Jonson had had five pitched battles with Shakspere:—*Every Man in* and *out of his Humour, Cynthia's Revels, Poetaster,* and the *Fox.* The following passage reminds us of *Cynthia's Revels,* where Fungoso is spoken of as delighting to make a fool of himself, and Crites calls him a jackdaw; of course it has reference to the name of Sir John Daw:—

> 3 *Ser.* "I'the city of kites and crows!—What an ass it is!—then thou dwellest with daws too?
> *Cor.*   No, I serve not thy master."
>
> Act iv., scene 5.

Iu Menenius we have our old friend John Lyly; that he is intended for a life-like portrait is evident from these extracts:—

> *Men.*   " I tell thee, fellow,
> Thy general is my lover: I have been
> The book of his good acts, whence men have read
> His fame unparallel'd."—Act v., scene 2.
> *Cor.*   " This last old man,
> Whom with a crack'd heart I have sent to Rome
> Loved me above the measure of a father;
> Nay, godded me indeed."—Act v., scene 3.

We are here reminded of the *Merchant of Venice:*—

> *Bass.* " The dearest friend to me, the kindest man,
> The best condition'd and unwearied spirit

In doing courtesies ; and one in whom
The ancient Roman honour more appears,
Than any that draws breath in Italy."

Act iii., scene 2.

The Dapper impertinence in the *Alchemist,* Shakspere
retaliates by laughing at Jonson as the rogue Autolycus
in the *Winter's Tale ;* and by painting him also as the
jealous Leontes, we are reminded of the translation of
Greene and Nash into Oberon and Puck. Shakspere
speaks chiefly through Polixenes and the clown.

Jonson and Inigo Jones acted together in producing
the *Masque of Queens,* February 2, 1609; and as Jones
appears to be satirised in the *Silent Woman,* it is just
possible, as he was architect to Prince Henry, and in
favour with King James, that Camillo is a representation
of that celebrated man, "of a nature generous and
noble." The good Polixenes bears evident marks of
being a portrait of good King James, and the observation, so objectionable to the Reverend Mr. Hunter, may
be a trait of his Majesty's hasty temper :—

" I am sorry, that, by hanging thee, I can but
Shorten thy life one week."

Act iv., scene 3.

Although, in 1610, Jonson produced the *Masque of
Oberon* and the *Barriers,* written to celebrate the
creation of Henry Prince of Wales on the 4th of June;
yet he did not take any part in the celebration of the
marriage of the Princess Elizabeth ; and it has been
remarked as a most singular circumstance, his muse is
silent on the death of Prince Henry ; and it appears, he
must have fallen into disgrace at Court about this
period :—

Aut. "I have served Prince Florizel, and, in my time,
wore three pile; but now I am out of service."

"I cannot tell, good sir, for which of his virtues it
was, but he was certainly whipped out of the court."—

Act iv., scene 2.

But in this romantic drama, as in *As You Like it,*
Shakspere's mind is again reverting to old times, and
in the character of Leontes he is thinking far more of
Greene than of Jonson. We are justified in this supposition by the comedy being founded on *Pandosto,* a
novel of Greene's, by the name of *Mamillius,* also taken
from another novel, *Mamillia;* there must also be some
definite meaning attached to the number (23) twenty-
three :—

Leon.   "Looking on the lines
Of my boy's face, methought I did recoil
Twenty-three years."
              "Twenty-three days
They have been absent: 'Tis good speed."

"Nine changes of the watery star" may denote, the
play was brought out nine months after the *Alchemist;*
and it must have been a recent production in May,
1611, since Dr. Forman noted it down so minutely in
his diary. If it was first acted in March or April,
twenty-three years would carry us back to 1588, when
Shakspere had a quarrel with Greene and Nash, and at
which time his son Hamnet was three years old, and
Greene had a son about twelve months younger; *Pandosto,* also, was first printed in 1588.

The following dates are equally precise and definite :—
Time, as Chorus, says, "Impute it not a crime, that I
slide o'er sixteen years;" and Camillo speaks of the

death of Hermione sixteen winters ago; but he had previously said, "it is fifteen years since I saw my country;" and yet he left Sicilia before Perdita. This difference in Camillo's measurement of time is most probably intentional, as well as characteristic of the forgetfulness of age; for as Jonson was married in 1594, he may have had a daughter in 1595, as he certainly had a son in 1596, in which year he also produced *Every Man in his Humour;* if Shakspere, then, really alludes to this period, it can only proceed from a most kind and conciliatory spirit, since it may be regarded as about the happiest portion of Jonson's life, whilst in the same year Shakspere's only son died, of whom Mamillius may be regarded as a tender and affectionate reminiscence, twin-brother to Arthur in *King John;* Shakspere had hazel eyes, but Mamillius has " a welkin eye," and Edward III. thus speaks of the Prince, his son:—

" His mother's visage, those his eyes are hers."

In Antigonus we meet again with our old friend Lyly,* whilst Paulina has all the tartness of Semele, and Leontes may justly look upon her as the wasp of all women. It should here be added, "the characters

---

* Lyly's honest old face is readily recognised peering through the thin disguise of the numerous characters of which he is the archetype, however distinct each individual may be. Shakspere seems to have made the same use, and as affectionately of him, as Vance did of the portrait of Sophy:—"I kept it as a study for my female heads— ' with variations,' as they say in music. Commencing as a Titania, she has been in turns a Psyche, a Beatrice Cenci, a Minna, a Portrait of a Nobleman's Daughter, Burns' Mary in Heaven, The Young Gleaner, and Sabrinafair, in Milton's *Comus.* I have led that child through all history, sacred and profane."—*What will he do with it,* Part xi.; c. 2.

of Antigonus, Paulina, Autolycus, and the young Shep-
herd, are the creations of Shakspere;"

On reading the beautiful description of the reconciliation of the two kings, so characteristic of the
forgiving spirit, of the noble and generous disposition
of the writer, we may reasonably suppose, all of Caliban
in Jonson's nature must have melted away before the
Miranda-like beauty of Shakspere; and it would be
pleasing to find, that amity was soon restored; but the
commentators keep up a continual cry about his malignant attacks and sneers against Shakspere; and this
Hue and Cry appears to be fully borne out in *Bartholomew Fair*, which was produced in 1614. But
before proceeding further, let us make a more minute
inspection of the ground already gone over, for in the
Winter's Tale we are reminded of the beautiful allegory
in *Twelfth Night*.

On looking into *Timon*, we find Alcibiades accom-
panied by two ladies, who, it is just possible, were
intended to represent Marston's comic and tragic muse,
or the two parts of *Antonio and Mellida*. Again, in
Othello, who is the lady so wondrous fair, the gentle
Desdemona? and who are Emilia and Biancha? When
honest Iago suspects the too great familiarity of the
Moor with his wife Emilia, malignant Ben confesses to
Shakspere's intimacy with the Grecian muse. And is
not the Moor's jealousy of Cassio the expression of
Shakspere's admiration of the *Malcontent*, his acknowledgment of Marston's genius, on whom his own love,
the romantic muse, has bestowed her sweetest smiles,
her warmest kisses, like *Cynthia* and *Endymion?* This

view of the allegorical imagery, concealed in *Othello*, is confirmed by the intimate connexion of that tragedy with the *Malcontent*, where Mendoza's too great familiarity with Aurelia is Marston's acknowledgment of Shakspere's classical acquirements. Who, then, is Ferneze, the young lover of Aurelia, whose death is caused by Mendoza's jealousy? And who is Roderigo, in love with Desdemona, and killed by Iago? who is this young lover, for the two must be one and the same person, who thus excites the jealousy of Shakspere and Jonson, or rather their love and admiration? perhaps we may find the solution in *Troilus and Cressida*.

This ' *Comical Satire,*' this most singular production, we now know is a supplement to *Othello*; consequently the *dramatis personæ* must have reference to the characters in the *Malcontent* and the *Poetaster;* and we shall find the poet had a method in his madness. According to Maginn, it is written in direct antagonism to the *Iliad*, and Gervinus says:—" It is remarkable, that Shakspere has in this play avoided confining himself closely to all his sources equally.—All the more important actions follow accurately no single source; the separate features of the story and of the characters, are disconnected, and are borrowed indifferently, if not intentionally, sometimes from one, sometimes from another.—Certain passages could only be derived from Homer himself."—*Vol.* 2, *p.* 303.

These extracts fully justify us in attributing to certain passages a hid sense, a special meaning. Consequently, by Hector's courteous language to Ajax and calling him

cousin,* Shakspere marks his friendly feeling to Marston,
and recognises him as a romantic poet; and when we
are told that Ajax "yesterday cop'd Hector in the
battle, and struck him down; the disdain and shame
whereof hath ever since kept Hector fasting and
waking," can we doubt, that Shakspere is alluding to
the *Malcontent*, a play at that time unrivalled in power
and intensity of passion save by his own *Timon*.. On
the other hand the abuse of Ajax would be a satire on
Marston's poetical style, his forced and turgid language.
When Troilus is spoken of as Hector's younger brother,
and "on him erect a second hope, as fairly built as
Hector," 'tis Shakspere confirming by anticipation the
critical opinion, that Fletcher is Shakspere's younger
brother: consequently when Ulysses slights Cressida,
'tis Shakspere's disapproval of young Fletcher's loose
and immoral muse. Fletcher was born in December,
1579, and therefore "had ne'er seen three and twenty
years" in the autumn of 1602. We can now under-
stand that Fletcher is shadowed in Ferneze and
Roderigo, and perhaps in Galeatzo, the young Prince of

---

* When Hector addresses Ajax :—
    "That thou could'st say—This hand is Grecian all,
    And this is Trojan; the sinews of this leg
    All Greek, and this all Troy; my mother's blood
    Runs on the dexter cheek, and this sinister
    Bounds-in my father's."—
                    Troilus and Cressida, Act iii., scene 5.

Shakspere must have had in his recollection :—
Ant. " O that I knew which joint, which side, which limb,
    Were father all, and had no mother in't,
    That I might rip it vein by vein, and carve revenge."—
                    Antonio's Revenge, Act iii., scene 3.

Florence in *Antonio and Mellida*. All the generals kissing Cressida, is probably a satire on the excessive osculation at that time, a pleasing custom grossly abused. The non-observance of this custom, the gentler and more polished manners of the Trojans, and Paris' Gallicism, "It is great day," raise a suspicion, Shakspere intended to shadow the French in the Trojans, possibly he may have had in his recollection the meeting at Boulogne, between Henry VIII. and Francis. We need scarcely add, that Helen is the Grecian muse.*

The three ladies in *Measure for Measure* appear also to be of an allegorical character; but in the *Tempest* we cannot doubt, Miranda, the daughter of Prospero, is the romantic muse, beloved by Ferdinand [Beaumont], son of Alonso [Chapman]. This view is confirmed by Jonson in the *Fox*, where Celia is the classical muse, so named after her in *As you Like it*. The characters of the honest, rough-tongued Chapman as Corbaccio, and of the amorous and loose-tongued Fletcher as Corvino, are very distinctly marked, and also Marston as Voltore, in the second scene of the fourth act, where Corvino swears he has seen the young Bonario [Beaumont], son of Corbaccio, warmly kissing and embracing his wife Celia. On this pretty conceit of the two poets, having

---

* It was a custom on the Elizabethan stage for a great actor like Burbage or Alleyn, to take two or three parts in the same play; and it was on this principle the comedy was constructed, but rather for reading than acting. According to the playbill, Jonson was engaged specially for Thersites, and also for Achilles and Menclaus;—Marston, specially for Pandarus, and also Patroclus and Ajax;—Shakspere, specially for Hector, and also Paris and Ulysses; Chapman performed Agamemnon, and Lyly, Nestor;—Troilus by Fletcher, and Diomed by Beaumont.

one muse in common, has been founded a story,
highly discreditable to the characters of Beaumont and
Fletcher; such is the sad result of attaching historical
value to idle anecdotes. The reader will now perceive
the probability, nay, the certainty that in Diomed was
shadowed the youthful Beaumont; at that time, in the
autumn of 1602, he was in his eighteenth year, it is
possible he may have assisted Fletcher in writing a
comedy, since he published a translation, or rather "a
huge paraphrase" from *Ovid* when only sixteen.

In *Lear*, Goneril and Regan may well represent the
muses of Decker and Marston; but be that as it may,
the once dearly-beloved Cordelia must be the romantic
muse. In her sad fate, hanged by the order of Edmund, and in the afflicting death of Lear, we have a
true and graphic image of the fate of Shakspere and his
muse, had he listened to Jonson's classical criticisms
and amputated his *drolleries* to the measure of Ben's
Procrustean bed. The rejection of Cordelia by the
Duke of Burgundy [Fletcher], and the eager acceptance
of her, as "a dowry in herself," by the King of France
[Beau-mont], distinctly mark Shakspere's estimation of
the two poets;— young Troilus had not paid attention
to Ulysses' opinion of Cressida. Could any biographical
value be attached to the liberality of Ferneze and
Roderigo, and to the dower-seeking of Burgundy we
should accede to the opinion, Fletcher inherited some
property but soon squandered it away. But in Ferdinand and France we have direct evidence that Beaumont was an ardent worshipper of the Shaksperian
muse; and, whilst his commendatory lines on the *Fox*

are a tribute to Jonson's vanity, Ferdinand carrying logs is an image of Shakspere's watchful care, and of the severe training of the youthful poet.

In *Macbeth*, by shadowing Marston in Banquo, Shakspere points at Fletcher in *Fleance* and we shall hereafter show good cause for this opinion.

We thus see, a poetical allegory is the vital principle, the delicate aroma, permeating these dramas; and in none is this ethereal essence more perceptible than in the *Winter's Tale* :—

> *Pol.*   " This jealousy
> Is for a precious creature : as she's rare,
> Must it be great; and as his person's mighty,
> Must it be violent; and as he does conceive
> He is dishonour'd by a man which ever
> Profess'd him, why, his revenges must
> In that be made more bitter."

Thus the jealousy of Leontes, like Iago's suspicion of the Moor, is another claim, made by Shakspere, of his intimacy with the Grecian muse; whilst in the marriage of Florizel and Perdita is shadowed the union of the Greek and romantic drama in the rising genius of Beaumont. Perdita's classical character is beautifully shown in her distribution of the flowers at the rustic feast.—We must now away from Fairy-land to the bitter trials of daily life.

In *Bartholomew Fair* Shakspere is delineated in the ridiculous character of Proctor Littlewit, " the Littlewit of London, so thou art called and something besides." The commentators have pointed out in the Induction a flirt at Shakspere and at *Much Ado about Nothing;*

and also a passage, in which the *Tempest* and the
Winter's Tale are sneered at:

" If there be never a servant-monster in the fair, who can help
it, he says, nor a nest of antiques? he is loth to make nature
afraid in his plays, like those that beget tales, tempests, and such
like drolleries."

The meaning of this passage is so clear and unmistakable, that nothing but wilful obstinacy could have
blinded Gifford, who will not see, that the learned Ben
Jouson is like Dr. Johnson, a classical bigot, and here
denounces two master-pieces of the romantic drama as
drolleries or puppet-shows; and further on, after a long
tirade of this " twice-sodden folly " attempting to make
black white, Gifford is forced to acknowledge, that
Jonson has caricatured Inigo Jones as Lanthorn
Leatherhead. Nor can it be doubted, Shakspere is
ridiculed not only as Proctor Littlewit, but also as Justice
Overdo and Squire Cokes. The malice of the Induction
denotes the pleasures of the Fair. We must not however omit Littlewit's account of his method of modern-
izing a Roman history:—" As for the Hellespont I
imagine our Thames here; and then Leander I make a
dyer's son about Puddlewharf; and Hero a wench o'the
Bankside." In March, 1613, Shakspere "bought a
house with ground attached near Blackfriars Theatre,
abutting upon a street leading down to Puddlewharf."

As Claudius died at the culminating point of his
iniquitous career just before Hamlet, so Jonson set
the seal to his own infamy just before Shakspere
died. In the *Devil is an Ass* Shakspere is grossly
ridiculed, and Daniel is no less grossly maligned; the

names of the characters are sufficient to condemn Jonson: Shakspere: Plutarchus Gilthead and Fabian Fitzdottrel; Daniel: Ever-ill; Jonson: Eustace Manly; and Inigo Jones: Engine; Chapman would be Sir Paul Eitherside, and Decker, Thomas Gilthead.

Plutarchus is clerk to Eitherside the lawyer, he is addressed, "my pretty Plutarchus," just as Tucca calls Ovid " my pretty Alcibiades;" the name is evidently an allusion to the Roman plays.

Fitzdottrel, a silly bird of the same feather as the Daw, makes his appearance as a Shakescene and a Crow in borrowed feathers: nor is Midas forgotten, he is both ass and ox; like Fungoso he is a friend to the tailor :—

> "What rate soever clothes be at; and thinks
> Himself *still new, in other men's old.*"
> > "out of the belief
> He has of his own great and catholic strengths
> In arguing and discourse."

The following lines are not less significant :—

Meer. "I think we have found a place to fit you now, sir, Gloucester,

Fitz. O no, I'll none.

Meer. Why, sir?

Fitz. 'Tis fatal.

Meer. That you say right in. Spencer, I think, the younger,
Had his last honour thence. But he was but earl.

Fitz. I know not that, sir. But Thomas of Woodstock,
I'm sure was duke, and he was made away
At Calice, as duke Humphrey was at Bury:
And Richard the Third, you know what end he came to.

Meer. By my faith you are cunning in the chronicle, sir.

Fitz. No, I confess I have it from the playbooks,
And think they are more authentic."

Meer. " To be
>   Duke of those lands you shall recover : take
>   Your title thence, sir, Duke of the Drown'd Lands,
>   Or Drown'd Land."

" This harmless passage about the playbooks, the commentators, Malone and Steevens in particular, are never
weary of recurring to with spiteful triumph; ' all Shakspere's historical plays are ridiculed' by the malignant
Ben." *Vide Gifford.*

These keen hounds however, notwithstanding Gifford's horror, were on the right scent; but not knowing
who Fitz was, they missed catching the fox, Volpone
himself. I have in the *Footsteps of Shakspere* explained
the line in Oberon's vision, " I saw but thou couldst
not," by the fact that Greene was, but Nash was not
born, when Queen Elizabeth ascended the throne; and
we have here a similar artifice ;—the observation about
Spenser is an allusion to Marlowe's play, *Edward the
Second*; consequently Fitzdottrel says, " I know not
that, sir;" but he knows the contents of his own plays,
and so naively adds, " I think they are more authentic."
This passage alone suffices to stamp Fitzdottrel as Shakspere. " I learn'd in it myself, to make my legs and do
my postures " proves, that Fitzdottrell is also a continuation of Asotus, the pupil of Amorphus; and the
witchcraft in the fifth act is Jonson's retaliation for the
character of Edmund in *Lear*.

But the whole gist of this Satanic comedy turns on
deluding Fitz with the hope of being his Grace the Duke
of Drown'd Land; a grand project that, strange to say,
never entered the head of Sir Politick Wouldbe tho'
dwelling in Venice; because the moral of the tale lies in

the fact, that in 1614 Shakspere " is found at this time busy about a project for the enclosure of the common fields of Stratford, and is consulted on that and other matters as the most public-spirited man in the town."

We thus see, how truly Hector's fate was a prefiguration of Shakspere's :—

> *Hect.* "Now is my day's work done : I'll take good breath :
> Rest sword : thou hast thy fill of blood and death !"

We here see the poet, retired from the stage, disarm'd, his sword " broken and buried certain fathoms in the earth," when " even with the vail and dark'ning of the sun to close the day up " comes Neoptolemus Jonson with his furious and malignant Myrmidons, *Bartlemy and the Devil* :—

> " Strike, fellows, strike ; this is the man I seek.
> On, Myrmidons ; and cry you all amain,
> *Ben Jonson** hath the mighty *Shakspere* slain."
> *Troilus and Cressida.*

The passage where Engine whispers Meercraft — " Do you remember the conceit you had of the Spanish gown at home," Act ii., sc. 3, has reference to Dame Pliant in the *Alchemist* and to the boy that acted Epicœne ; and further on we read :—

> *Meer.* "Sir, be confident,
> 'Tis no hard thing t' outdo the Devil in ;
> A boy of thirteen year old made him an ass
> But t'other day."
> Act v., sc. 3.

---

* *Pie.* "It shall be chronicled, time to come:
Piero Sforza slew Andrugio's son."
Antonio and Mellida, Act iii., p. 43.

As the *Silent Woman* was produced in 1609 and *Every Man in his Humour* in 1596, it follows the boy must have been Jonson's own masculine muse, which, dressed as a lady, Shakspere [Sir John Daw] mistakes for the Grecian muse; the allegory is perfect, keenly satirical, well worthy of a wit larded with malice; nor can we doubt that Dol in the *Alchemist* is a caricature of the romantic muse, whilst Dame Pliant, married to Lovewit (Jonson), is intended for the classical muse.

This passage proves, that Meercraft is Jonson; for how could Meercraft know anything about the *Silent Woman* and the *Alchemist*, unless he were a continuation of one of the characters or the author himself. It appears, that Meercraft is the same as Face in the *Alchemist*; since it is Face, who proposes to Subtle to marry Dame Pliant to the Spaniard; consequently Subtle is the same person as Engine, and must be a satirical stroke at Inigo Jones :—

Face.   " 'Tis his fault;
            He ever murmurs, and objects his pains,
            And says, the weight of all lies upon him.—
            Hang him, proud stag, with his broad velvet head."
                                    Alchemist, Act 1., sc. 1.

As Subtle says to Face, "Here's your Hieronymo's cloak and hat," it follows, Face and Meercraft are in reality the author; whilst Manly and Lovewit are fictitious characters, which he wishes to impose on the public as portraits of himself; and as the *Fox* and *Alchemist* are two plays of similar construction, it can scarcely be doubted, Mosca is the precursor of Face.   Let Shakspere and Jonson be testimonied, as the Duke says in *Measure*

for Measure, by their *bringings forth ;*—Jonson is happiest and most at home in painting gulls and describing
the tricks of rogues ; whilst Shakspere "in deep delight
is chiefly drowned " in dwelling on characters, of which
there is scarcely a trace to be found in Jonson's works;
and which said works, or bringings forth, fully bear out
Drummond's character of him, "a dissembler of ill
parts which rayne in him, a bragger of some good that
he wanteth." Thus at the end of the *Alchemist,* Lovewit
profits by the rascality of his servant, and therefore
forgives him; then Face comes forward requesting a
plaudite from the spectators: precious teaching of
morality ! our sympathies enlisted on behalf of a clever
rogue and a receiver of stolen goods, or at least obtained
under false pretences.

We must receive with some caution the statements of
Gifford, who instead of being the dispassionate bio-
grapher, sinks himself into the blind advocate. It is
both possible and probable Daniel may have spoken un-
favourably of Jonson ; but the character of Everill does
not fit in with Jonson's words, "he bore him no illwill
on his part." We have evidence that Shakspere in 1614
was busy about a project for the enclosure of the common fields of Stratford; and in 1616 Jonson, in opposi-
tion to Daniel, was made Poet Laureat;—in the *Devil
is an Ass,* written probably about Christmas, 1615, is a
Fiztdottrel, Duke of Drown'd Land, of the same family
as Fungoso, Asotus, and Sir John Daw, whilst Everill is
a candidate for the office of Master of the Dependances,
and makes to a lady similar insinuations against Manly,
as Daniel is said to have made against Jonson ; such
cincidences are rarely accidental.

It was easy for Jonson in 1623 to praise the dead
lion, but we can have little confidence in his sincerity in
placing above the classic tragedians of Greece the
romantic dramatist, author of those two drolleries, the
Tempest and the *Winter's Tale*; nor can we place much
reliance on his almost idolatrous affection; it would
seem rather, both his praise and affection are a tribute
to public opinion. These suppositions are confirmed by
his statements to Drummond, and more especially in the
Staple of News, 1625, where Jonson ridicules Shakspere
as Pennyboy junior, in fact, a reproduction of Asotus in
love with Lady Argurion; and in January, 1629-80,
when the New Inn was "completely damn'd" not being
heard to the conclusion, if he had loved and respected
the memory of his *friend*, would he have vented his ill-
will on the "malicious spectators" by a sneer not only
at *Pericles* but also at *Love's Labour's Lost* :—

> "No doubt some mouldy tale,
>   Like Pericles and stale."
> "For who the relish of these guests will fit,
>   Needs set them but the alms-basket of wit."

In the *New Inn* Jonson amuses himself with ridiculing
Shakspere as Fly, and Inigo Jones as Sir Glorious
Tipto, evidently an imitation of Don Armado and Moth.
This play was the cause of the subsequent hostility of
Inigo Jones, and not the trivial circumstance of Jonson
having put his name first on the title-page of a masque.

On looking back to the origin of this contest we find,
the first effect of Jonson's action on the Shaksperian
drama was the cutting short of the earthly career of Sir
John Falstaff, which Shakspere intended to have con-

tinued in *Henry V.*; but his path was crossed by a spectre, *monstrum horrendum, informe*, which Sir Toby Belch ridicules with Falstaffian humour in *Twelfth Night*, and hence Sir John is quickly despatched in *Henry V.*, that "you be not too much cloyed with fat meat."

In *Much Ado about Nothing* we again see the dark'ning influence of Jonson, a comedy filled with the materials and verging on tragedy; whilst the beautiful and romantic drama, *As you Like it*, is penetrated with the spirit of the melancholy Jaques:—

> " Blow, blow, thou winter wind,
> Thou art not so unkind,
> As man's ingratitude."

But these fleecy clouds, casting a melancholy shade over bright Cynthia, soon aggregate together, and in *Timon* the storm bursts forth. Jonson is the spark, or rather the sulphurous match, that has ignited the combustible elements of those three volcanic eruptions, *Timon*, *Othello*, and *Lear*. In these dramas we see, how the celestial influences of *Cynthia* are disturbed by the terrestrial motions of malignant Ben;—the more the lion roars, the more does *Ursa major* dance;—the more our gentle Willy groans, the more does Macilente grin; and when Phœbe in *As you Like it* exclaims:—

> " Dead shepherd! now I find thy saw of might;
> *Who ever lov'd, that lov'd not at first sight?* "

'tis the breathing forth of a sigh for poor Marlowe back again, and Jonson in his place.

But it would be a grievous error to regard this dramatic contest as a mere personal quarrel. Although

Jonson is in each instance the aggressor, yet Shakspere in his reply, however indignant, only points at Jonson in certain characters; and, though he gives some home-thrusts, and tells some bitter truths, he no-where delineates the man himself, unless Iago be he. These dramas, from first to last, are essentially æsthetical productions; or perhaps it may with still greater truth be said, they fully bear out the opinion of Ulrici, who connects the action and characterization of Shakspere's dramas with the development of a high moral or rather Christian principle.

As Beaumont and Fletcher were not only frequenters of the *Mermaid*, but also on friendly terms with Jonson, it becomes highly interesting to see what light they throw on this contest; and as those persons, who may take an interest in this inquiry, will of course refer to the Plays, I shall confine myself chiefly to pointing out the various characters.

The Knight of the Burning Pestle is generally supposed to have been brought upon the stage in 1611;—it is directed against the absurdities of the earlier drama, more particularly those of Heywood's *Four Prentices of London,*—written about the close of the preceding century. It is also said to have been " the elder of Don Quixote above a year," meaning, it is assumed, the translation in 1612. Such may be a just interpretation of the dedication to the first edition, 1618, on which however much reliance cannot be placed, as it was not written by either poet, and the publication may have been piratical,

But, whether acted or not, this comedy, at least the

first sketch, appears to have been composed in 1604, and singularly too the elder of Don Quixote above a year, the first part of which Cervantes did not publish before 1605 ; this opinion is supported by the following allusions, which in 1611 must have been somewhat out of date :—in the Induction or prologue the Citizen says,—" *These seven years* there hath been plays at this house, I have observ'd it, you have still girds at citizens;" and the Wife remarks of Ralph,—" Nay, gentlemen, he hath played before, my husband says, *Musidorus*, before the wardens of our company." This play, *Musidorus*, was printed in 1598; and the *Four Prentices of London* " was written about the close of the preceding century,"perhaps in 1597; and old Merrythought's remark, " how have I done these forty years," may refer to Shakspere's birth year.

Although the *Knight of the Burning Pestle* appears to have been written in ridicule of the *Four Prentices of London* and of knight-errantry, it also bears evident marks of being a satirical attack on Jonson as the originator of *Eastward Hoe :*—Old Merrythought : Lyly ;—Jasper, his son, apprentice to a rich merchant : Shakspere ;—Ralph, knight of the Burning Pestle : Jonson ;—Humphrey, the merchant's friend : Chapman ;— and Michael, the second son of old Merrythought : Marston.

Jasper, apparently an idle apprentice, but really an excellent young man, runs away with Luce, the merchant's daughter, encounters and conquers Ralph :—

> *Jasp.*   Come, Knight, I'm ready for you, now your pestle
>   [*snatches away his pestle.*
> Shall try what temper, sir, your mortars of."

Jasper, pretending to die and being carried to the merchant's house in his coffin, is evidently borrowed from *Antonio and Mellida,* and justifies the supposition, Michael may be intended for Marston; and when the wife says of Jasper:—" He's e'en in the highway to the gallows, God bless him;" and again, " Go thy ways, thou art as crooked a sprig as ever grew in London, I warrant him, he'll come to some naughty end or other;" we are reminded of Slit in *Eastward Hoe:*—" Look, what a sort of people cluster about the gallows there! in good truth it is so. O me! a fine young gentleman! What, and taken up at the gallows! Heaven grant he be not one day taken down there! A my life it is ominous."—Act iv., sc. 1.

If the characters of the Merchant, Humphrey, Jasper and Luce were written by Beaumont, and old Merrythought and Ralph by Fletcher, we need not be surprised at Beaumont being painted as Ferdinand in love with Miranda, nor at Fletcher having a niche in the *Fox* as Corvino.

The Mad Lover. Memnon, the boasting general and Mad Lover: Jonson;—Polydor, brother to Memnon: Shakspere;—Chilax, an old merry soldier: Lyly;—Syphax: Marston;—Eumenes, Polybius, and Pelius, three Captains: Beaumont, Fletcher, and Decker.

Throughout these plays the female characters appear to be allegorical; the princess Calis, *the beautiful,* is the romantic muse, with whom Jonson is desperately enamoured, and also Marston, but Shakspere in this instance carries off the prize. Polydor's remedy for Memnon's love reminds us of young Freewill and his

unhappy friend Malheureux in the *Dutch Courtezan*;
Memnon, however, like Malheureux, saves his virtue.
Polydor in his bier, like Jasper, is of course borrowed
from *Antonio and Mellida;* these imitations or borrowings from Marston force on us the opinion, that Syphax
is intended for Marston, and his marriage with Chloe
may be an allusion to the marriage of Lucio in
Measure for Measure. As Chilax says, " these twenty-
five years I have serv'd my country," and as *Euphues*
was published in 1580, it follows, the *Mad Lover* may
have been produced in 1605 after the appearance of the
Fox, being a burlesque on the quarrel between Shakspere
and Jonson. This play is attributed to Fletcher, but
I opine, the same hand that drew Jasper and Luce, must
have drawn Polydor and Calis. In these two plays the
muse of Fletcher is truly a very indelicate Cressida.

The Woman-hater is another comical satire on the
three authors of *Eastward Hoe.* The Duke of Milan is
Shakspere, in love with Oriana, the sister [muse] of
Count Valore [Beaumont]. Gondarino, *the woman-
hater* : Jonson; Arrigo, a *courtier :* Lyly; Lucio, a
weak formal statesman : Chapman ; Pandar is of course
Marston ; and the mercer, Decker ; Lazarillo, a *volup-
tuous Smell-feast*, is certainly Fletcher, who, like many
of his brethren, is as ready to wear motley as to put the
foolscap on others ; and accordingly Lazarillo tells us
his age :

Dnke. " How old are you ?
Laz.   And eight and twenty times hath Phœbus' car
          Run out his yearly course since."

As this comedy was licensed in May, 1607, Fletcher

being then in his twenty-eighth year, we cannot doubt
of the person intended. In the opening of this comedy
the author must have had in his recollection the first
scene of the *Malcontent*, and from the following lines we
infer Fletcher must have written a comedy in 1599,
praising Shakspere and satirising Jonson:—

> *Val.* " Let me entreat your grace to stay a little,
> To know a gentleman, *to whom yourself*
> *Is much beholding :* He hath made the sport
> For your whole court these eight years, on my
> knowledge." Act ii., sc. 1.

It has been shown we have reason for believing
Fletcher is intended by Ferneze in the *Malcontent*, and
it becomes probable, he was afterwards ridiculed as
Caqueteur, *a prattling gull*, in the *Dutch Courtezan*:—

> *Cri.* " Sir, I'll no more 'a your service—you are a child—
> I'll give you my nurse."
> Act iii., sc. 1.

Fletcher must have had a great admiration for Marston, and, though no imitator, he has borrowed from him
the burlesque sublime ; and there are good grounds for
the belief, that in his tragic efforts also he followed
toiling in the wake of Marston.

This comedy, the *Woman-hater*, acted in 1606, fully
justifies and may have been the cause of Fletcher being
pointed at in *Fleance* as the future king of poesy; a pro-
phecy singularly fulfilled, since he was for nearly half a
century regarded as the greatest poet and dramatist,
even for a time overshadowing the name of Shakspere.

Philaster. The King of Sicily and Calabria, *an
Usurper*: Chapman ; Pharamond, Prince of Spain:
Jonson ; Philaster, *rightful Heir to the crown*: Shaks-

pere; Dion : Lyly; Cleremont and Thrasiline : Fletcher and Beaumont.

Throughout the play Philaster has numerous traits of Hamlet, "alas, he's mad;" and scenes are ingeniously devised to throw him into similar positions and passions with Hamlet. Jonson speaks of his almost idolatrous affection for Shakspere, but this play is one of the purest pieces of idolatry poet ever offered ; and when Dion, speaking of Philaster's retort to Pharamoud, says,— " H'as given him a general purge already," Beaumont must have had in his recollection the passage in the *Return from Parnassus,*—" O, that Ben Jonson is a pestilent fellow ;—but our fellow Shakspere hath given him a purge that made him bewray his credit."

This is a beautiful and romantic drama, and needs no allegory ; but there seems to be one in the two ladies ; —Arethusa, a river of Greece, flows under the sea and rises again in Sicily (England) ; that is, the Grecian muse, buried during the middle or dark ages, re-appears in Chapman's translation of the *Iliad,* who is enthroned, as in the *Poetaster*, king of the English poets, and wishes to transmit his sceptre to the learned Jonson, but he is clearly an usurper. Shakspere is the heir of Dan Chaucer, and by Philaster's marriage with Arethusa is intimated, he was well read in Greek, Homer, and the Tragedians.

This play is assigned to 1608 or '9 ; and it must have appeared before the *Silent Woman,* for Jonson with the tact and instinct of malice has transferred Thrasiline and Cleremont bodily into that comedy under the names of Sir Dauphine Eugenie and Cleremont ; and Dauphine

may he a reminiscence of the King of France in Lear.
But that is not all ; for Epicœne or the *Silent Woman* is
a boy, a trick of Sir Dauphine's, and the whole comedy
is a satire or parody on *Philaster*; the *eclaircissement*
at the end being the *denouement* of each play.

The Custom of the Country. For the ingenious piece
of malice in representing them as sneering at their
friends, Shakspere and Inigo Jones, as Sir John Daw
and La Foole, our two poets repaid Jonson by painting
him in this comedy as Duarte, *a gentleman well qualified
but vain-glorious* :—

> " an excellent scholar and he knows it ;
> An exact courtier, and he knows that too ;
> He has fought thrice, and come off still with honour,
> Which he forgets not."
>
> Act ii. sc. 1.

No one can mistake the picture, a striking likeness,
and the date in the corner, Christmas, 1609, as Rutilio
(Fletcher) says, " I have lived this thirty years." Jonson is also satirised as the villainous-looking bravo, who
had committed three murders, and would rather kill a
man than maim him, as dead men tell no tales. Leo-
pold, a sea-captain, in love with Hippolyta : Marston ;—
Arnoldo : Shakspere ; Charino, father of Zenocia : Lyly ;
Alonzo : Beaumont. Having thus given the retort
courteous to Jonson our poets proceeded in a less satirical mood to—

The Maid's Tragedy. As Amintor, *a noble gentleman,*
is a similar character to Prince Philaster, this play must
also be regarded as another tribute of respect to Shakspere. King of Rhodes : Marston ; Jonson : Melantius,
who talks largely but not such a boaster as Memnon ;

Amintor thus speaks of him, reminding us of Fuller's account of the wit combats at the *Mermaid :—*

> *Amin.* " What vile wrong
> Has stirred my worthy friend, who is as slow
> To fight with words, as he is quick of hand ?"
> Act i., sc. 1.

Calianax, *an old humourous lord,* and father to Aspatia: Lyly; Cleon and Strato: Beaumont and Fletcher.

We may judge from the following imitations in the *Winter's Tale,* how highly Shakspere admired this tragedy, and how deeply he was affected by the delicate flattery therein,—an offering far more grateful and sweet-smelling than the idle puff of commendatory verses :—

> *Lys.*   " when she sees a bank
> Stuck full of flowers, she with a sigh will tell
> Her servants what a pretty place it were
> To bury lovers in ; and make her maids
> Pluck 'em, and strew her over like a corse."
> *The Maid's Tragedy,* Act i., sc. 1.
> *Per.*   " O, these I lack,
> To make you garlands of ; and my sweet friend,
> To strew him o'er and o'er.
> *Flo.*   What, like a corse ?
> *Per.* No, like a bank, for love to lie and play on ;
> Not like a corse."
> *Winter's Tale,* Act iv., sc. 3.

There is also a similar passage in *Philaster,* Act iv., sc. 4.

Melantius thus addresses Calianax :—

> *Mel.* I shall forget this place, thy age, my safety,

And through all, cut that poor sickly week,
Thou hast to live, away from thee."

        The Maid's Tragedy, Act i., sc. 1.

Pol.   " Thou old traitor,
I am sorry, that, by hanging thee, I can but
Shorten thy life one week."

        Winter's Tale, Act iv., sc. 3

The allegorical character of the two ladies in this tragedy is very distinctly marked ; for the one is named after Evadne, who slighted the addresses of Apollo ; and the other, not after the celebrated Aspatia of Athens, but the mistress of Cyrus, priestess of the sun, famous for her personal charms, elegance, and beauty of complexion.   Euphrasia in *Philaster* is said to be an imitation of Viola, but Aspatia is Viola herself,—" patience on a monument smiling at grief :"—" strive to make me look like sorrow's monument;" and when Aspatia, dressed in her brother's clothes says, " 'tis twelve years since I saw my sister," 'tis an allusion to *Twelfth Night*, which was composed in the autumn of 1598.

About the time this tragedy was produced, Jonson brought out the *Alchemist,* in which he takes his revenge for the satire in the *Custom of the Country* by ridiculing Fletcher as Drugger, *a Tobacco-man*, and Beaumont as Kastrill *the angry boy*.   Our poets replied in

The Humourous Lieutenant.   In this comedy Jonson is caricatured as the Lieutenant, and satirised as King Antigonus, *an old man with young desires*.   Prince Demetrius, *his son, in love with Celia :* Shakspere.   Two Gentlemen, *friends and followers of Demetrius :* Beaumont and Fletcher.   Seleucus is probably Chapman, and Lysimachus and Ptolemy may be Marston and Decker.

—Leontius, *a merry old soldier :* Lyly. As Leontius says, " I have not wept this thirty years and upwards," the play may have been written in the autumn of 1610.

The Lieutenant having a regiment of children whom he'll "unbeget and knock 'em on the head if disobedient," may be an allusion to Jonson's *sons.* His wonderful love and admiration for the king after drinking the potion is not only a satire on Jonson's servile adulation of King James, but also on his excessive vanity, reminding us of Sir Andrew laughing at Malvolio's vain and affected airs in *Twelfth Night.*

Although this play is universally given to Fletcher, and, no doubt, the characters of Leontius and the Humourous Lieutenant were by him, yet, I suspect, the scenes more immediately connected with Celia were written by Beaumont. Not only may we be sure, he would repay Jonson for *the angry boy* in the *Alchemist,* but this play readily divides into two parts only slightly held together by one or two scenes.

In 1611 Jonson brought out *Catiline ;* but as the tragedy is so purely classical, containing no personal satire except inferentially, our poets complimented Jonson thereon in commendatory verses ; Beaumont's however have evidently a satirical smack. They may then have spent eight days in refiling and polishing *The Knight of the burning Pestle,* which, however, bears a very juvenile look by the side of the *Humourous Lieutenant,* between it and the noble play they next proceeded to, or—

King and No King ; in which, however, the second scene in the second act may have been suggested by the earlier comedy, Philip being a second edition of Ralph. Arbaces (Jonson) is a mighty conqueror and braggart, takes Tigranes (Shakspere) prisoner in single combat; but treats him kindly, promising him his only sister in marriage and says of him :—

> " This prince, Mardonius,
> Is full of wisdom, valour, all the graces
> Man can receive.
> *Mar.* And yet you conquer'd him."

Evidently the character is a comical satire. This speech and the remark of Mardonius remind us of Pharamond and Thrasiline in the opening of *Philaster*.

The single combat, the dubiousness of Arbaces' birth, and his mother attempting to poison him, are well-known allusions to Jonson. Panthea, the supposed sister of Arbaces, with whom he falls desperately in love and afterwards marries, is intended, as her name, *all-divine*, denotes, for the classical muse; whilst Spaconia, beloved by Tigranes, is the romantic muse. Gobrias: Chapman; Lygones, *father of Spaconia* : Lyly; Bacurius : Inigo Jones; Mardonius : Beaumont; whilst Fletcher amuses himself by acting the part of Bessus, *the lying coward*, and then by a date fixes the caricature on Jonson,— " but in a cudgell'd body, from eighteen to eight-and thirty;"—this play having been licensed in 1611, thirty-eight years will carry us back to 1573, in which year Jonson was born; and possibly he went to the Low Countries in 1591; and Bessus says, " I think I have been cudgell'd with all nations and almost all religions." Bacurius degrading Bessus by taking his sword from him may be an allusion to Inigo Jones, who was probably the means of getting Jonson dismissed from the service of Prince Henry; and Lygones beating Bessus, twinging his nose and kicking him, may be a retaliation for the twinges by the nose and the kicks *sans nombre* given to Sir John Daw and La Foole.

The following dates appear to have a peculiar significancy;—" She (Panthea) but nine years old I left her, and ne'er saw her since," says Arbaces; and Gobrias tells him, " you grew up as the king's son, till you were six years old; then did the king die, and—left this queen truly with child, indeed of the fair princess, Panthea." In these dates Beaumont appears to be paying a high compliment to Fletcher's muse, as well as to Jonson; we may presume, Panthea is in her sixteenth year, born in 1596 and last seen by Arbaces in 1605, complimentary allusions to *Every Man in His Humour*, and to the *Fox*; so far Panthea is the supposed sister or Jonson's own muse. But Fletcher was six years younger than Jonson, consequently Arbaces' admiration of Panthea would be a pleasing allusion to Jonson's commendatory verses on the *Faithful Shepherdess*, the rightful princess and Queen of " Iberia."

Notwithstanding the acknowledged difficulty of deciding what scenes or passages may have been written by either poet, yet there seem good grounds for attributing particular scenes to Beaumont. Thus the discourse between Arbaces and Mardonius in the first act reminds us of the friendship between Beaumont and Jonson; again from *Enter Arbaces, &c.* to *Exeunt Kings*, Act ii., sc. 2, must also be by him, since the passage closely resembles the end of *Philaster*; whilst the con-

test in the mind of Arbaces on account of his love for
Panthea is just the mental analysis Beaumont delights
in; consequently we have no hesitation in attributing
to him the characters of Arbaces, Tigranes, Mardonius,
Panthea, and Spaconia; and to Fletcher the scenes in
which Bessus is a principal character,—Mardonius would
be common to both poets.

We cannot doubt, that Beaumont wrote Arbaces and
Tigranes, since in the *Triumph of Honour in Four Plays
in One,* universally ascribed to Beaumont, Martius and
Sophocles are similar characters; and this *Triumph*
must have been written soon after the *Winter's Tale,*
since Sophocles (Shakspere) says, " Seven times have I
met thee face to face;"—*Every man in* and *out of his
Humour, Cynthia's Revels,* the *Poetaster,* the *Fox,* the
Silent Woman, and the *Alchemist;—Sejanus* was a con-
joint production.

The Scornful Lady may have followed *King and No
King,* and we presume from various passages, the same
hand that drew the *Lady,* also painted Celia in the
Humourous Lieutenant. Of the plays written in 1612-
13 we shall at present only notice—

The Knight of Malta.—After looking through this
play the reader would immediately pronounce Miranda,
the Knight of Malta and pure soldier of the cross, to be
Shakspere; Gomera, *a deserving Spanish gentleman:*
Jonson; and Mountferrat, *a Knight of the Order, but
a villain:* Marston; Valetta, *the Grand Master:* Chapman; Colonna *alias* Angelo: Decker; Norandine, *a
valiant and merry Dane:* Lyly; Astorius and Castriot,
two Knights of the Order: Beaumont and Fletcher.

This explanation rests on the following items;—the remark of Miranda, " Boy, did he call me? Gomera call me boy?" links Gomera and Miranda with Aufidius and Coriolanus. The character of Gomera is a copy of the jealous Leontes; in fact Gomera and Oriana may be regarded as an imitation of Leontes and Hermione in the *Winter's Tale*.

This drama appears to have been produced in the autumn of 1612, since Lucinda is " a virgin of fourteen," which connects her with Viola in *Twelfth Night*, whilst Gomera and Miranda having served " full ten years," that is, made war against the Turks, may be an allusion to Othello. Again in the opening of the play, Mountferrat says, " full sixteen years " fortune and victory have been his servitors; this led me at first to suppose the character was a satire on Jonson, but the unmistakable imitation of Marston's style shows the poet's meaning :—

" The wages of scorn'd love is baneful hate;"
whilst Zanthia, Oriana's maid, is the same treacherous creature as Zanthia in *Sophonisba*; and Oriana, like Sophonisba, is also described as the wonder of women.

Consequently Marston must have produced some remarkable work in 1596; and it would seem, his satires were written in that year though not published till 1598; for it turns out, the *Knight of Malta* is founded on, or is a reply to the *Insatiate Countess*; in which tragi-comedy Marston and Jonson appear as Signior Claridiano and Signior Rogero, with their wives (muses), Abigail and Thais, " fourteen years called sisters;" and it follows, the play was produced in 1610.

Isabella, the tragic muse, marries Count Roberto (Shakspere); and at a masque on the bridal-night she falls in love with Count Guido (Beaumont), and runs away with him the next morning; soon after she transfers her affections to his friend Count Gniaca (Fletcher). Roberto, shocked at the depravity of his wife, retires to a monastery, and is a similar character with Miranda, the *Knight of Malta;* whilst Mendosa and Lady Lentilus are the prototypes of Angelo and Lucinda; Duke Amago: Chapman.* Read by this light the *Insatiate Countess* is sufficiently amusing, half satirical and half complimentary to Beaumont and Fletcher on the success of *Philaster* and the *Maid's Tragedy.* Guido satirising Isabella as the *insatiate* countess may be allegorical of Beaumont's devotion to the tragic muse at that period. The following points are also noteworthy; Abigail says, her husband has written "an ungodly volume of satires against women, and calls his book *the Snarle.*"—The remark of Thais, " I should have my husband *pliant* to me," may be an allusion to Dame Pliant in the *Alchemist,* to this particular expression:—

> *Sub.* " Pray God, your sister prove but pliant."—
> *The Alchemist,* Act iv., scene 2.

Thais also calls her husband "the Knight of the supposed Horne." Gniaca says, "women-haters now are common;" and "less the cities powers rise to rescue him " may indicate, that Webster is shadowed in Colonel Sago. That some definite meaning is attached

---

* In Marston's Works the *Insatiate Countess* is unfortunately a mere reprint of an old edition; and amongst other errors the name of Rogero is repeatedly misprinted for Guido, making a sad confusion.

to these several phrases we may surmise from the remark of Rogero, " Why now I see thou lovest me," which is a quotation from Chapman's *Bussy D'Ambois,* where Monsieur, after the friendly contest of personal abuse, says to Bussy, " Why now I see thou lovest me."

The Knight of Malta is generally attributed to Fletcher, and he appears to have written the scenes, in which Mountferrat, Zanthia, and Norandine are the principal characters; but all the scenes connected with *Miranda* I should give to Beaumont.

The Two Noble Kinsmen.—This play is supposed to have been written by Shakspere and Fletcher, but the only external evidence is the title of the first edition, 1634, and " a tradition of the playhouse, that the first act only was wrote by Shakspere." The play readily divides into two parts, very slightly connected together. Theseus, Hippolyta, and Emilia, are by the hand of Beaumont;—the underplot by Fletcher.

Arcite is Shakspere; and Palamon, Jonson; their characters are very distinctly drawn, the noble and conciliatory spirit of the one as opposed to the tetchiness and irritable jealousy of the other. The knight described on the side of Arcite must be Sir Walter Ralegh, or the Moor, " his complexion *nearer a brown than black;*" the first on the side of Palamon is Carr, Earl of Somerset, who was in his twenty-fifth year in 1614; the other knight æt. 36, may be Sir Thomas Coventry, who was born in 1578; their characters correspond with the descriptions of the poet, but I can find no account of Sir Thomas' personal appearance; he was " Counsel for the Crown in the trial of the Somer-

sets,—but either *from his own inclination*, or the
jealousy of the King's Serjeant and the Attorney
General, he did not act a conspicuous part in any of
them."—*Lives of the Chancellors*, Vol. ii., p. 513.

In Theseus and Hippolyta are shadowed Chapman
and his Homeric muse, and Creon, "a most unbounded
tyrant," uncle to the princes, is the terrible Marston.
Emilia is the goddess of poetry; Palamon wins her by
the death of Arcite,—that is, Shakspere having retired
from the service of the muses, Jonson remains first poet
of the age. The Jailor's Daughter, in love with Palamon, being eighteen, fixes the date of the drama, 1614.

Beaumont wrote the first act; the sixth scene of the
third act, from '*Enter Theseus*,' &c.; the second scene
in the fourth act; the first, second, third, and fifth
scenes, and from '*Enter Pirithous*' in the sixth scene
of the fifth act. Thus the scenes, essentially classical
and forming *a perfect poem, not a word in excess nor a
word wanting*, appear to have been written by Beaumont, and thus this beautiful Anglo-Greek drama,
Theseus and Hippolyta, nearly the last production of his
genius, remains a monument to his own glory, and a
mausoleum for the manes of Shakspere and Jonson.
The description of the battle, instead of the battle itself
on the stage, being a direct imitation of the Greek
tragedy, and the language throughout so thoroughly
Shaksperian, confirms the allegory in the *Winter's
Tale*, where Beaumont is represented as the son of
Shakspere, married to the Grecian muse. By the early
death of Beaumont we lost an English Sophocles, whose
Æschylus was glorious John Marston, he! that fronted
Shakspere, as Ajax "cop'd Hector."

There now comes a change over the scene; this play, the *Two Noble Kinsmen*, so flattering to Jonson, must have been written in the spring of 1614, and with equal certainty we can say, *Rollo, the Bloody Brother*, was written in the autumn of the same year; and we have no hesitation in attributing to Fletcher the impassioned scenes between Rollo and Edith, whilst Beaumont drew the character of the good Aubrey [Chapman], whose age, "about fifty-seven," gives the date of the tragedy; and whilst Shakspere is shadowed in the gentle Otto, Marston is satirised as the Bloody Brother, and Jonson as Latorch, ' Rollo's earwig.'

This tragedy appears to have been followed by *The False One*, in which Jonson is satirised as the villain Septimius; Shakspere is pointed at in Pompey, whilst Marston would be Cæsar, and Chapman, Achoreus; Antony, and Dolabella, Cæsar's *Captains :* Fletcher and Decker; Ptolemy: Beaumont; and by a singular coincidence, this is the only play in which his representative character dies. In this play the first act appears to have been written by Beaumont, all the rest by Fletcher, probably in consequence of the death of Beaumont. The play is named the *The False One*, not after Cleopatra, but after Septimius :—

> *Sept.*   " Since I in my nature
> Was fashioned to be false."
> *Ant.*   " There's no doubt then
> Thou wilt be false."—
>
> Act v., scene 3.

Nor is it improbable, Carr, Earl of Somerset, is shadowed in Photinus, for the following lines remind us

of Jonson's congratulatory epistle to the Earl on his
marriage in 1613 :—

  Sept. "You are my god on earth ! and let me have
          Your favour here, fall what can fall hereafter.
  Pho. Thou art believed ; dost thou want money ?
  Sept. No, sir.
  Pho. Or hast thou any suit ? These ever follow
          Thy vehement protestations.
  Sept. You much wrong me :
          How can I want when your beams shine upon me,
          Unless employment to express my zeal
          To do your greatness service."—
                     The False One, Act i., scene 1.

  "They are not those, are present with their face,
    And clothes and gifts, that only do thee grace
    At these thy nuptials ; but whose heart and thought
    Do wait upon thee ; and their love not bought."—
                     Jonson to Carr.

The severity of the satire in these two tragedies, un-
mitigated as in other plays by a complimentary character,
justifies the supposition, there must have arisen a quarrel
between Beaumont and Jonson, and the cause may have
been *Bartholomew Fair* ; wherein we find two friends,
Winwife and Quarlous, contending for the love of Grace
Welborn, who has the same difficulty, as Emilia, in
choosing between her two admirers, and in the pocket-
book Quarlous writes Argalus, and Winwife, Palemon ;
we cannot then doubt that in this scene Jonson had in
his recollection the *Two Noble Kinsmen ;* Winwife
(Beaumont) wins the lady, whilst Quarlous (Fletcher)
marries Dame Purecraft for her money, because "it is
money that I want."

To what extent the quarrel may have proceeded,

whether beyond a mere dramatic contest, Beaumont and Fletcher taking up the cudgels for Shakspere, we cannot pretend to decide, but it is certain, notwithstanding the intimacy and friendship between Beaumont and Jonson, and the appearance of the *Two Noble Kinsmen* in 1614, Jonson wrote no elegy on the death of his friend in 1616, but brings out, whether before or after the death of Shakspere may be dubious, the *Devil is an Ass*; in which comedy Beaumont and Fletcher are represented as Wittipol and Trains. Wittipol reminds us of Sir Dauphine in the *Silent Woman*, and is so named after Wittipate in *Wit at several Weapons*, and Pug is probably borrowed from Antonio in the *Coxcomb* :—

Wit. " How now ! what play have we here ?
Man. What fine new matters ?
Wit. The coxcomb and the coverlet."

Act v., sc. 5.

And when Manly says, " I should know this voice and face too," we are reminded of Viola in the *Coxcomb,* " I know that voice and face," and also of Maria, " Ha ! I should know that jewel ; 'tis my husband."

We need not then be surprised at the wrath of Beaumont and Fletcher on seeing their humourous and kindly effusions transformed into illnatured satire, and themselves into sneerers at their best and dearest friend, the man they idolized. After the death of Beaumont, Fletcher carried on the war against Jonson with undimished vigour, lampooning him as " a malicious Beautefeau," in the *Queen of Corinth,* 1616, where the characters of Theanor and Crates remind us of Photinus and Septimius ; and the expression, " On, my Engine, on," must be an allusion to the *Devil is an Ass.*

In these plays and in all where his hand is traceable
the muse of Beaumont is most chaste, decorous, an
moral, whilst Fletcher, though he often delights us a
Cupid, not seldom offends as a satyr. Nor can it b
doubted, many of the female characters are allegorical
this is most apparent in the selection of the names c
Arethusa and Evadne, and especially in the character o
Emilia in the *Two Noble Kinsmen*; but notwithstanding
this allegorical nature there is a richness and fullness i
their characterization we in vain seek for in late
dramatists; the same fullness of life appears also in th
comedies of Marston and others at that period; and a
Philip in *Northward Ho* says, his father regarded th
nine Muses as so many beautiful women, it must b
acknowledged, in the days of Elizabeth and James th
English muse was a buxom lass, healthy and vigorous
the child of nature, native to the soil;—but the cold
classical, and Frenchified poets* of great Anna and th
eighteenth century stript the goddess of her flesh an
blood, and sent *the delighted spirit* to wander about th
earth like a Werther wailing;—since then, 'tis said, sh
had been seen in America and in England had on th
helmet of Arthur; but, be that as it may, 'tis certain
she loves Garibaldi and dwells in the hearts of th
British volunteers, guarding the throne of Victoria,—
that is her home.

As Webster not only added some scenes to the *Malcontent*, but also joined Decker in writing *Northwar*
Ho, and *Westward Ho*, let us now examine—

---

* This is very evident in Congreve's *Double Dealer*, which, though
brilliant and sparkling as champagne, is a most watery dilution, Hah
neman's thirtieth attenuation, of *Cynthia's Revels* and *Othello*.

The Duchess of Malfi. After reading this tragedy we cannot doubt, Bosola is intended for Jonson; and yet beyond the character so graphically drawn as if by Shakspere's own hand, there is not a trace, not the slightest evidence justifying such a suspicion;—nor is there any more cause for supposing that the good and noble Antonio, steward to the Duchess and privately married to her, is Shakspere, a character applicable to him only as farmer and manager, and yet one closes the book with the conviction, Antonio and Bosola are Shakspere and Jonson.

Webster wrote two tragedies about the same period, and they appear to be connected together in the author's mind; for the heroine of the one is a bad woman, the White Devil; whilst the Duchess of Malfi is an angel of purity. Now in the preface to the first play, *Vittoria Corombona*, or the White Devil, the following passage precludes the supposition the author intended any personality in the play against either Shakspere or Jonson; and yet they are perhaps even more appositely represented by the two brothers, Marcello and Flamineo, than by Antonio and Bosola in the other play :—

"Detraction is the sworn friend to ignorance; for mine own part, I have ever truly cherished my good opinion of other men's worthy labours ; especially of that full and heightened style of Master Chapman; the laboured and understanding works of Master Jonson; the no less worthy composures of the both worthily excellent Master Beaumont and Master Fletcher ; and lastly [without wrong last to be named], the right happy and copious industry of Master Shakspere, Master

Decker, and Master Heywood; wishing what I w
may be read by their light; protesting that, in
strength of mine own judgment, I know them so wort
and though I rest silent in my own work, yet to m
of theirs I dare [without flattery] fix that of Martial
    "Non norunt hœc monumenta mori."
Under such circumstances it becomes highly imp
bable, that any personal allusion could have b
intended in the *Duchess of Malfi*. But on looking i
the *White Devil* to our astonishment we discover, t
the seven leading personages in the tragedy correspo
exactly with the characters of the seven poets mentio
in the preface; and that the passage just quoted is
more a clue than a blind to the author's meani:
"*wishing what I write may be read by their ligh*
Monticelso: Chapman; the two Dukes, Francisco a
Brachiano: Beaumont and Fletcher; the two broth
Flamineo and Marcello: Jonson and Shakspere; Lo
vico and Camillo will then be Decker and Heywo
Beaumont is admirably drawn as Francisco, the gr
plotter, and the following lines may be a satire on his f
quent use of thunder in *Philaster :*—

> *Fran.* "Look to 't, for our anger
>   Is making thunderbolts.
> *Brach.*   Thunder! in faith,
>   They are but crackers."

The quarrel between Brachiano and Isabella is e
dently an imitation of the eclaircissement between Evad
and Amintor. But how comes it, that Marston's nam
omitted in the preface, for on the second page there
a quotation from the *Parasitaster*, and Zanche,

Moorish chambermaid, is the same as Zanthia in *Sophon-isba*. This singular omission leads to the supposition, that Vittoria, the sister of Flamineo and Marcello [Jonson and Shakspere], must be Marston's fierce and lustful muse; whilst in Brachiano's passionate love for this White Devil is painted Fletcher's admiration of Marston's genius.*

But behind these dramatists there appears to be some historical figures;—in Brachiano and Vittoria are fore-shadowed the loves and marriage of the Countess of Essex and Carr, afterwards Earl of Somerset. The arraignment of Vittoria is a most open imitation of the trial of Sir Walter Ralegh, and when Francisco says, "the act of blood let pass; only descend to the matter of incontinence," we are reminded of the *Main and the Bye;* consequently Francisco, disguised as a Moor, must stand for Sir Walter; and this disguise confirms the supposition, Shakspere in *Othello* had an eye to Ralegh.

---

* This poetical enthronement of Marston's muse justifies the opinion that in the *Insatiate Countess* Webster is represented in the character of Colonel Sago, the best beloved of Isabella the tragic muse. This must be a complimentary allusion to some previous tragedy, probably to *Appius and Virginia*, where Marston appears to be shadowed in Appius Claudius, 'a huge rascal' in the play, but allegorically a com-plimentary character, since Marston is here again contending with Shakspere (Icilius) for Virginia, the classical muse; but Jonson is represented in Marcus Claudius, a base wretch, that can neither poetically nor allegorically be twisted into a respectable character. Chapman would be the noble Roman, Virginius, and hence the date:—As Virginia is fourteen, born after her father had been married fifteen years, and as the supposed child of Marcus' bondwoman would be *Every Man in his Humour*, it follows, this tragedy was brought out in 1610 : and further that Chapman produced his first play in 1596, after having been married to the muses fifteen years;—his first comedy was published in 1598.

The following lines clearly point at *Othello* and the
expeditions against Cadiz and the Azores in 1596 and '7

> *Flam.*   " I have not seen a goodlier personage,
> Nor ever talk'd with men better experienc'd
> In state affairs or rudiments of war :
> He hath, by report, serv'd the Venetian
> In Candy these twice-seven years, and been chief
> In many a bold design."

Giovanni is evidently a portrait of Prince Henry.

We may now return to the *Duchess of Malfi*; the
following extract clearly marks Bosola as Jonson; he
continually protests his honesty, and is only a villain
through circumstances ; he dies however repentant :—

> *Ant.*   " Here comes Bosola,*
> The only court-gall ; yet I observe his railing
> Is not for simple love of piety :
> Indeed, he rails at those things which he wants ;
> Would be as lecherous, covetous, or proud,
> Bloody, or envious, as any man,
> If he had means to be so."
>
>   Act i., sc. 1.

But far differently does Webster speak of Antonio
[Shakspere], describing him as " a complete man," and
applying to him the closing lines of the play, that
" Integrity of life is fame's best friend."

On a more minute examination these two tragedies
prove, Webster was an ardent student of the Shaksperian drama; that he loved the man and worshipped
his muse. In that most poetical scene in the *White
Devil*, where Cornelia and her ladies are "discovered
winding the corse of Marcello," the scene opens with

---

* Webster had probably in his mind the lines of Timon to Apemantus,
and of Isabella against Angelo in *Measure for Measure*.

an imitation of Ophelia's distraction and also of Lady
Macbeth's sleeping soliloquy, followed by a dirge, of
which C. Lamb says, " I never saw anything like this
dirge except the ditty which reminds Ferdinand of his
drowned father in the *Tempest.* As that is of the water,
watery; so this is of the earth, earthy. Both have that
intenseness of feeling, which seems to resolve itself into
the elements which it contemplates."

These and other recollections or borrowings from
Shakspere are not to be regarded as denoting a poverty
of fancy;—far from it; they are the delicate flatteries
which, instead of commendatory verses, "the right
happy and copious industry" of Master Webster and
Beaumont, &c. offered to the princely autocrat of the
stage; and when in *Cymbeline,* in imitation of the dirge
over the body of Marcello, a song is sung at the grave
of Fidele, 'tis not a stolen idea, a poverty of invention,
but a graceful recognition of Webster's devotional
offering; for was not Marcello, Shakspere? *Tu Mar-
cellus eris.*

If then Webster had this holy reverence for the genius
of Shakspere, can it be doubted, that in the *Duchess of
Malfi* are allegorized the sufferings of the Shaksperian
muse from the persecutions of Jonson; and assuredlly
had Shakspere cramped his genius to the critical dimen-
sions of Ben, it would have been as effectually throttled,
as was the Duchess by Bosola. From the remark of
Ferdinand we may infer, Beaumont was born the very
day *Pericles* was first acted :—

Ferd. " She and I were twins ;
　　　And should I die this instant, I had liv'd

Her time to a minute."
                              Duchess of Malfi, Act iv., sc. 2.

Whilst the Duchess may be regarded as the tragic
muse, Julia is the comic muse, married to Castruccio
(Heywood), beloved by Delio [Decker], and now
bestowing her smiles on the Cardinal (Fletcher).

There appears to be a bit of secret history in these
two plays, having reference to a particular period of
Jonson's life,—on the death of Brachiano the young
duke Giovanni [Prince Henry] immediately orders
Flamineo " to forbear the presence and all rooms that
owe him reverence ;" and Flamineo remarks, " he hath
his uncle's (the Moor's) villainous look already." Jonson fell into disgrace at court (*vide Winter's Tale*), about
Christmas, 1610, at latest, and remained so till after the
death of Prince Henry and the marriage of the Princess
Elizabeth. He also had at one period a quarrel with
Sir Walter, and kindly told Drummond, that " Ralegh
esteemed more fame than conscience; the best wits of
England were employed in making his *History of the
World*."

From this intimate connection between these plays it
may be conjectured, the *Duchess of Malfi* was composed about Christmas, 1613; and it becomes highly
probable, the prologue to *Every Man in his Humour* was
re-written by Jonson for the sake of venting his spite
upon this play and the *Tempest*.

The story, that there had been a quarrel between
Chapman and Jonson about this period, appears to be confirmed by a passage in Act iii., sc. 3, where Delio says,
the great Count Malatesti " hath read all the late ser-

vice, as the City Chronicle relates it." Chapman was joined with Inigo Jones in producing the masque at the marriage of the Princess Elizabeth, to which the above extract may refer. The Marquis of Pescara is Marston; Delio is Decker; and Castruccio, Heywood; Duke Ferdinand and his brother, the Cardinal, are Beaumont and Fletcher. We gather from their plays, that Beaumont and Fletcher, being of a cheerful and sanguine temperament, rather enjoyed the fight between Shakspere and Jonson; and being also free from jealousy, idolizing the one, and respecting the powerful intellect of the other, they joined in the melée with a joyous heartiness void of malice and offence; but Webster, being of a graver and more serious disposition, disapproved of these follies, and regarded it as a desecration to approach Shakspere otherwise than with love and reverence.

Perhaps one of the most ingenious methods of tormenting the Duchess of Malfi was letting loose a set of madmen in her chamber; another remarkable scene is the madness of Duke Ferdinand; and it has been shown Webster had great reverence for Shakspere;—now on looking into *Bartholomew Fair* we find a lunatic, Trouble-all, who has a prodigious reverence for Justice Overdo; but such a harmless joke would be poor revenge on the part of Jonson, so Webster is also satirised as Zeal-of-the-land Busy, suitor to Dame Purecraft.— Squire Cokes is another character in this comedy, under which Shakspere is ridiculed; and Cokes is carefully watched and attended upon by Humphrey Waspe,* a humourous caricature of Chapman, who seems to have

---

* A reminiscence of Kent in *Lear*, who was also put into the stocks.

been a warm tempered old gentleman, and through life
almost as warmly attached to Shakspere as Lyly was.

On turning back to the *Alchemist*, in which both
Beaumont and Fletcher are ridiculed, we find two
characters similar to Waspe and Zeal-of-the-land
Busy; it may then be surmised, Chapman and Webster are therein satirised as Pertinax Surly and
Tribulation Wholesome; whilst Ananias, a Deacon, may
be intended for Decker, who sometimes wrote jointly
with Webster. As Webster in the preface to *Vittoria
Corombona* says, he was a long time in finishing the
tragedy, it may be regarded in some measure as a reply
to the *Alchemist*, and brought out about Christmas,
1611 ; and we thus obtain a very clear view of this contest. Jonson brings out in the summer of 1609 the
Silent Woman, Shakspere replies in *Coriolanus* in the
autumn : and Webster supports him, as a volunteer
early in 1610 with *Appius and Virginia*; in which
tragedy Virginius would be Chapman; Numitorius:
Inigo Jones ; Minutius : Lyly ; Icilius : Shakspere;
Appius Claudius: Marston ; and Marcus Claudius:
Jonson. The *Alchemist* and the *Maid's Tragedy* appear
in the summer, the *Insatiable Countess* in the autumn,
and whilst Webster is elaborating his masterpiece, the
Winter's Tale comes out in the spring of 1611. After
this long ramble we must now return to Shakspere.

In *Julius Cæsar*, notwithstanding his close adhesion
to Plutarch, Shakspere must have had in his recollection
the sad fate of the Earl of Essex. This opinion is
justified by the circumstance, that in *Macbeth*, written
in the previous year, the earl's death is shadowed in the

Thane of Cawdor. Such being the case, Cæsar would be Essex; Brutus and Cassius: Bacon and Coke; Antony: Anthony Bacon; and Cicero: Cecil. But be that as it may, the figures of certain dramatists shine clear and distinct through these ancient Romans.

In Julius Cæsar we recognise the mighty Marston; Brutus and Cassius are Shakspere and Jonson, confirmed by the imitation of their contention in the *Maid's Tragedy*; and Casca would be Decker; and who does not see in Octavius and Antony, Beaumont and Fletcher? and we have previously shown, that in the *False One* Marston and Fletcher appear as Cæsar and Antony.

But it may be asked, how could Shakspere represent himself in Brutus as guilty of ingratitude to Marston? for the very plain reason, that in *Sophonisba*, only a few months previously, Marston had painted him as the noble Massinissa, and the ghost of Asdrubal was the earthquake, that shook Shakspere to his centre and awoke *Macbeth*; hence the ghost of Banquo, and hence the ghost of Cæsar in the tent of Brutus, where Shakspere deserts his Plutarch, but with the highest artistic skill and psychological knowledge; for the "horrible and monstrous spectre" must have been in the o'er-wrought mind of Brutus the shade of Cæsar, calling itself to his restless conscience his "evil genius;" and such appears to have been Shakspere's meaning, since Brutus, just before the appearance of the spectre, says, "O murd'rous slumber! Lay'st thou thy leaden mace upon my boy, that plays thee music?" Was not the mind of the gentle Brutus brooding on another *mur-d'rous slumber?* and with his last breath he exclaims,

" Cæsar, *now be still*; I kill'd not thee with half so
good a will." Thus does our poet in this drama as in
others by his wonderful art and magic power weld all
things to his will.

The immediate incentive to Julius Cæsar was the
publication of the *Fox* in February, 1607, with a dedication to the two Universities, which, considering the
circumstances under which the *Fox* was composed, must
be regarded as an insidious attack on the ignorant Shakspere, who replied to the challenge by this noble drama.

Antony and Cleopatra was probably produced in the
following year; and it has been shown in the " Sonnets
re-arranged," that the principal characters correspond
with the characters in the Sonnets; nor after a most
minute inspection can there be found in this play the
slightest trace of Jonson; neither Lepidus nor
Pompey can be tortured into a malignant Ben and still
less Cæsar. This fact indicates, the author must have
had some other special object in view; for in all the
other plays, *in every one*, since 1598, Jonson holds a
conspicuous position.

But in *Coriolanus* Jonson re-appears, and there cannot be a doubt, we have here three Richmonds in the
field :—Coriolanus, Shakspere, and Ralegh, all three in
one ; the characters may be thus arranged :—

Coriolanus.	Shakspere.	Ralegh.
Aufidius.	Jonson.	————
Titus Lartius.	Beaumont.	Essex.
Cominius.	Fletcher.	L. Admiral Howard.
Menenius.	Lyly.	————
Sicinius.	Jonson.	————

In the opening of the play the inefficiency of the two generals, and the brilliant deeds of Marcius in Corioli, and in the field, remind us of Ralegh at Cadiz *practically* superseding the two commanders, rivalling in heroic achievements Marcius Coriolanus, and well deserving a similar addition to his name as knight of Cadiz.

The evidence that Shakspere had an eye on Ralegh in the first act, rests entirely on the variations from Plutarch, which apparently refer to the expeditions against Cadiz and the Azores. According to Plutarch, Marcius enters Corioli, not alone, but " with so small a number, that summoning all his force he performed the most incredible exploits, which afforded Lartius an opportunity to bring in the rest of the Romans unmolested ; " and Marcius on joining Cominius merely requested to be opposed to the Antiates, "esteemed to be the warlikest men."

The words of Lartius, " I'll lean upon one crutch, 'ere *stay behind* this business," may be an allusion to Essex ;* and the observation of Brutus, " *O, if he had borne the business*," to Ralegh.† And again, " Re-enter Marcius *bleeding*," may be an allusion to Ralegh going in his skiff to Essex. And it is said, " Ralegh, to his great honour, held *always single* in the head of all."

The account of Lartius in Corioli, " busied about

---

* ".It appears that he had been impatient to be gone, for fear he should be detained, for the Queen had persuaded him to *stay behind ;* but not prevailing, she now gave him liberty to depart."—*Oldys.*, p. 238.

† " They presently possessed his lordship's head, that Ralegh had taken this opportunity to play over his parts, and shew the world how well he could act the conqueror, only to steal honour and reputation from the general."

108

decrees, ransoming and threatening," refers to Essex and the generals in Cadiz; and the following lines to Ralegh's admirable conduct after the battle :*—

> *Mar.* " Where is the enemy?   Are you lords o' the field?
> If not, why cease you till you are so ? "

We have in this play several remarks, trifles light as air, but of singular significance on being brought together and examined in the lump ;—thus Aufidius says, " Five times, Marcius, I have fought with thee ;" and again,† " Thou has beat me out twelve several times ;" and Sicinius is addressed as, " Thou Triton of the minnows," and "hadst thou foxship ;" Menenius says, " We call a nettle but a nettle," speaks of Coriolanus as his son, and says, " thy general is my lover ;" who in return speaks of Menenius as loving him " above the measure of a father : nay, godded me indeed ;" whilst the servants fear, lest this hero be cannibally given, and should broil or roast their master.

From this analysis of *Coriolanus,* we are justified in the belief, Shakspere has here given us another instance

---

* " He had desired the consent of the generals, that he might go and secure or destroy the Indian fleet ; but they desired to consider on it till next morning. At break of day Ralegh sent again, but the generals sent back to desire he would come ashore into the town.—The next morning, being the 23rd of June, the Duke of Medina caused all that fleet of merchantmen to be set on fire, because he was convinced, from their being beset so vigilantly by Ralegh, who had the charge of them, that they must needs fall into his hands."—*Oldys.*

† *Every Man in* and *out of his Humour, Cynthia's Revels, Poetaster,* and the *Fox.—Twelfth Night, Henry V., Much ado about Nothing, As you Like it, Timon, Othello, Troilus and Cressida, Measure for Measure, Tempest, Lear, Macbeth, Julius Cæsar.*

of his admiration and sympathy for the heroic prisoner in the tower.

Furthermore, can any one have a doubt, that Shakspere had Ralegh in his mind's eye in the character of Ventidius.—*Antony and Cleopatra*, Act iii., scene 1. The remark of Ventidius about being the revenger of M. Crassus' death, may refer to Ralegh at Cadiz attacking the St. Philip, to revenge the destruction of the Revenge. Cæsar and Antony are evidently the Lord Admiral and Essex; and the remarkable expression, "when him we serve's away," as well as the passage about Sossius irresistibly force on us the conviction, that Shakspere is alluding to Ralegh at Fayal.

As Ralegh was satirised in *Eastward Hoe*, and as *Coriolanus* is a reply to the *Silent Woman*, it may be reasonably conjectured, that Captain Otter is a caricature of Sir Walter, especially when we consider how distinctly he is pointed at in the *White Devil*. Besides the Cadiz expedition and the Island voyage, are mentioned at the end of the first Act in the *Silent Woman*; and it may be added, Ralegh was born on the banks of the Otter.

Considering the frequent and fierce disputes between Shakspere and Jonson, it becomes highly improbable, Jonson should have written either prologue, epilogue, or the supposed interpolation in Cranmer's speech in *Henry VIII*. On comparing the last page of *Cymbeline* with Cranmer's speech, the reader will perceive not only similarity of expression but also of feeling. Nor should it be forgotten there is not one word of personal adulation to the king; for though Elizabeth is called a

Phœnix and a Sheba, James is not even called a Solomon.

But who, it may be asked, is Cymbeline? and who is Imogen?

On reading this play, soon after the *Winter's Tale*, the feeling continually haunted me, I was once again wandering in fairy-land; that, if not the whole, at least much of it is allegory; "Hark! hark! the lark at heaven's gate sings," sends us at once back again to the happy days of our youth, to the merry meetings at the *Mitre*, to dear old Lyly and the fairies kissing Endymion. But I could find no clue to the mystery, no "open sesame," no Aladdin's lamp; till on coming to the end of the play, suddenly what in me was dark, "the beams o' the sun" illumined:—Cymbeline is a poet's free-will offering on the marriage of the Princess Elizabeth with Frederick, Count Palatine, on Valentine's day, 1613 :—

> *Sooth.* " The fingers of the powers above do tune
> The harmony of this peace. The vision
> Which I made known to Lucius, ere the stroke
> Of this yet scarce-cold battle, *at this instant*
> Is full accomplish'd : For the Roman eagle
> From south to west on wing soaring aloft,
> Lessen'd herself, and in the beams o' the sun
> So vanish'd : which foreshadow'd our princely
> eagle,
> The imperial Cæsar should again unite
> His favour with the radiant Cymbeline,
> Which shines here in the west."
>
> *Cym.*   Set we forward : Let
> A Roman and a British ensign wave
> Friendly together ; so through Lud's town march :

And in the temple of great Jupiter
Our peace we'll ratify; seal it with feasts."

The Roman eagle, vanishing in the beams of the sun
shining in the west, would mean, in a common-sense
view, the annihilation of the Roman army, which has
just occurred; but the Soothsayer does not allow of
such an interpretation, we must therefore seek another
solution; the Count Palatine, an elector of the German
empire, of the imperial Cæsar, is the Roman eagle; he
was, like Posthumus, far below the Princess in rank,
and Queen Anne was very indignant at the match, and
afterwards vented her spleen by calling the Princess
"goody Palsgrave;" such conduct smacks a little of
Cymbeline's queen; by this splendid alliance the Count
Palatine is absorbed into the royal family of England,
of the sun shining in the west.

Cymbeline is King James, and no doubt his Majesty
appropriated to himself:—"the radiant Cymbeline,
which shines here in the west;" but it is not probable
he applied to himself Cymbeline's tendency to favouritism
and peace at any price, consenting to pay tribute to the
Romans after having defeated them.

Cloten appears to be more a portrait than a satire on
Rochester, the king's minion, and he is also described,
like Carr, as a remarkably fine built man.   And we are
of necessity compelled to believe, we see in Imogen, if
not the Princess Elizabeth herself, at least the language
and manners of a young lady of high rank in 1612.

Imogen is not only the Princess Elizabeth, the Pearl
of Britain, as the Germans called her, but she is also
the goddess of the romantic drama, Shakspere's own

muse; and on seeing her wondrous beauty, the classical
Roman, Jachimo, exclaims :—

> " All of her, that is out of door, most rich !
> If she be furnish'd with a mind so rare,
> She is alone the Arabian bird."

The words of Posthumus to Jachimo are remarkable,
and deserve notice, since there are grounds for believing
Shakspere intended this play to be his farewell to the
stage, and his deliberate answer to the address, "To the
Reader," prefixed to the *Alchemist* in 1612, or Jonson's
criticism on the *Winter's Tale :—*

> *Post.*   " Kneel not to me ;
> The power that I have on you, is to spare you,
> The malice towards you to forgive you : Live,
> And deal with others better."

" On the 16th October, 1612, Ferdinand V, the Count
Palatine, arrived in England to receive his young bride.
In the midst of the festive preparations for this marriage, Prince Henry was seized with a dangerous illness,
and, it seems, one morning *his attendants thought him
dead, the prince, however, recovered from his faint,* and
in the afternoon took two cordials or nostrums, one of
which was prepared and sent by the captive Ralegh, who
had devoted a great deal of his time to chemistry; on
one occasion, when the Queen was very ill, she took his
draught, and experienced immediate relief."

It may then be presumed, in the good physician
Cornelius we see a delicate compliment to Ralegh, who
is, however, more strikingly depicted as Belarius, whom
Shakspere certainly intended for a good character;"
and "*I stole these babes*" is a shot fired at Sir Edward

Coke, who during Ralegh's trial, sought to fix upon him "those words of *destroying the king and his cubs*." Shakspere here again, as in the *Tempest*, stands up and avouches the innocence of Sir Walter:—

> *Bel.*　　　　　　　　　　"I, old Morgan,
> Am that Belarius whom you sometime banish'd:
> Your pleasure was my mere offence, my punishment
> Itself, and all my treason; that I suffer'd,
> Was all the harm I did."—Act v., sc. 5.

Whilst Prince Charles is traceable in the gentle Arviragus, Prince Henry is still more distinctly marked in the bolder Guiderius. The Count Palatine deserved the praises bestowed upon the noble Posthumus:—

> " Liv'd in court,
> [Which rare it is to do,] most prais'd, most lov'd;
> A sample to the youngest."

The long separation of Imogen from her husband, with her wandering in boy's clothes and dying of poison, corresponds remarkably with the postponement of the nuptials of the Princess, during which period her brother died; so the song sung at the grave of Fidele is Prince Henry's fairy knell:—

> " Fear no more the heat o' the sun,
> 　　Nor the furious winter's rages;
> Thou thy worldly task hast done,
> 　　Home art gone, and ta'en thy wages:"

and yet it is written again and again, " neither on the occasion of the marriage of the Princess Elizabeth, nor when there was a 'voice of weeping heard and loud lament,' on the death of Prince Henry, and when almost every poetic voice was raised, Shakspere *is not to be found*." 　.

Although Lyly holds a prominent position both in *Coriolanus* and the *Winter's Tale*, he is not to be found in *Cymbeline*, but "hark! the lark at heaven's gate sings" sounds like a requiem o'er his tomb; nor does he appear in any play by Beaumont and Fletcher during the twelve months following the *Knight of Malta*; it may then be surmised, Lyly died in the autumn of 1612.

As *Cymbeline* appears to have been a dramatic representation of the royal family, and as in the *Winter's Tale* Autolycus is certainly Jonson, so Florizel must be Prince Henry; and consequently Shakspere was, to the great distress of Mr. Armitage Brown, "a servile flatterer," or as Dr. Johnson has it, "he knew his trade;" still it is singular, that with such a good sprag memory, he should only have learnt his business at the eleventh hour; probably his morals had been corrupted by the example of that fulsome flatterer, malignant Ben, the honestest fellow in all Bohemia;—but who, then, is Perdita? who stood prototype to that fair shepherdess? the very name suggests the hapless fair, the Lady Arabella:—"Gentle and affectionate, she delighted in the refined pursuits of literature, in the elegant arts, which give a zest to retirement, and in the society of a few chosen friends, with whom she could indulge dreams of romantic felicity."

In that allegorical age, the allusions in these two romantic dramas, without being personal, would be readily felt and understood;—King James would approve of Cymbeline and the good Polixenes; Prince Henry, in his eighteenth year, would sympathise with Florizel and dream of a Perdita; Arabella would sympathise with Perdita, and see in Florizel her faithful Seymour; whilst the Princess might recognise herself in Imogen, weep over the grave of Fidele, and see in the noble Posthumus her dearly-beloved Count Palatine;—so far, I believe, Shakspere was a flatterer; so far, he knew his trade.

The critics have pointed out a passage in *Cymbeline*, " the ruddock would with charitable bill—," which Webster is supposed to have imitated; Steevens has also noticed some beautiful lines similar to, " Why, he but sleeps;" the supposition, however, of such imitations having been made by Webster is untenable, as the *White Devil* was published in 1612; it must, then, be granted, these imitations are by Shakspere, and consequently, the whole death-scene of Fidele is a Shaksperian imitation of the *winding* of Marcello. And further, it should be noted,—not only the latter lines in *Cymbeline*, but also the similar ones in *Henry VIII.* are imitated, in each play, directly from *Philaster* :—

Bel.   " These two fair Cedar-branches
       The noblest of the mountain, where they grew,
       Straitest and tallest."

     " Till never-pleased Fortune shot up shrubs,
       Base under-brambles, to divorce these branches ;
       And for a while they did so."

King. " That you may grow yourselves over all lands,
       And live to see your plenteous branches spring
       Where-ever there is sun ! "—
                   Philaster, Act v.

     " The lofty cedar, royal Cymbeline,
       Personates thee : and thy lopped branches,"—
                   Cymbeline Act

> " Wherever the bright sun of heaven shall shine,
> His honour, and the greatness of his name
> Shall be, and make new nations : He shall flourish
> And, like a mountain cedar, reach his branches
> To all the plains about him."—
>
> Henry VIII., Act v., scene 4.

There are also similar lines in *King and no King*, Act ii., scene 2.

And who can Philario be, the mutual friend of Jachimo (Jonson) and of Posthumus (Shakspere), but Beaumont, a compound of Phil-aster and Bell-ario? And why does Posthumus, in the last scene, strike the page [*striking her, she falls*], but because Philaster wounds both Arethusa and Bellario? And is not the passage :—

> *Jach.*   " could this carl,
> A very drudge of nature's, have subdued me,
> In my profession,"—

a reminiscence of—

> *Phil.* " The gods take part against me, could this Boor
> Have held me thus else ? "—
>
> Philaster, Act iv.

The passionate speech of Posthumus at the end of the second act is a reminiscence of Albano's speech at the end of Marston's *What you Will;** and

---

* The good Albano is Shakspere ; Randolph and Andrea, Albano's brothers : Beaumont and Fletcher ; Lampatho Doria : Marston ; Quadratus : Jonson ; Simplicius Faber : Decker ; the Schoolmaster may be intended for Lyly ; Jacomo and Laverdure ; two humourous satires on Jonson and Shakspere. Lampatho Doria is acknowledged to be the author himself, and Quadratus thus describes him :—

> *Quad.* " I protest, believe him not ; I'll beg thee, Laverdure,
> For a conceal'd idiot, if thou credit him ;

the sanguine star on the neck of Guiderius, and the mole on Imogen's breast, must have been intimately connected in Shakspere's mind with the mark on Albano's breast :—

> *Alb.* " I, good, good; come hither, Celia.
> Burst breast, rive heart a sunder! Celia,
> Why startest thou back? Seest thou this, Celia?
> O me! how often, with lascivious touch, thy lip
> Hath kiss'd this mark? How oft this much-wrong'd breast
> Hath borne the gentle weight of thy soft cheek?
> *Cel.* O me, my dearest lord,—my sweet, sweet love! "
> *What you Will*, Act v., p. 294.

There is a still more apposite speech by Albano in the third act, p. 256. The latter part of Posthumus' speech is most likely a reminiscence of Mendoza's abuse of women in the second scene of the *Malcontent*.

In this wonderful drama, filled with the warmth, splendour, and glory of the westering sun, Shakspere's farewell to the stage, a long farewell to all his glory, what can these numerous imitations mean, so open and undisguised, unless they are our poet's thanks, his acknowledgment and acceptance of the incense offered him by Beaumont, Fletcher, Marston, and Webster.

> He's a hyena, and with civet scent
> Of perfum'd words, draws to make a prey
> For laughter of thy credit."—Act ii., scene 1.

Consequently, Lampatho is the self-same character as Carlo Buffone in *Every Man out of his Humour*, and this fact gives a consistency to the opinion, that the phrase, "thou grand Scourge," was not a mere allusion, but was used intentionally by Jonson, to fix on Marston the satire of Carlo Buffone,—"a public, scurrilous, and profane jester, that more swift than Circe, with absurd similes, will transform any person into deformity."

Throughout the play, the allegorical imagery is most
exact and singularly pleasing;—Imogen, the romantic
muse, mistaking the body of Cloten for her lover's, and
with her own hands going to bury it, is a tribute of
respect to Marston * and not to Carr; whilst her ready

---

* We have seen that Marston and Essex are shadowed in Julius
Cæsar, that both were satirised in Alcibiades; but whilst in the magnificent extravagance of Timon, Shakspere may have had Essex in his
view, in the fierce denunciations to Alcibiades Marston stood before
him, or *Antonio's Revenge,*—a portrait of Hamlet by Marston, as *Philaster* was another by Beaumont; Antonio and Timon, Mendoza and
Othello, ghost of Asdrubal and ghost of Banquo, these are the indis-
soluble bonds between Marston and Shakspere. It was the kindred
lightning-flash of Marston's genius, even more than the satanic sneer of
Jonson, that roused the slumbering energies of Jove, made him shake
his ambrosial locks, and hurl the fiery bolt.

We must not, however, forget the amusing comedy of the *Parasitaster,* or Marston's parody on the *Tempest;* at least the characters
of Tiberio and Dulcimel are written, as Maginn might say, in direct
antagonism to Ferdinand and Miranda; Dulcimel is also, like Miranda,
fifteen; and Granuffo and Gonzago remind us of Alonzo and Gonzalo.
Hercules, Duke of Ferrara: Shakspere; Tiberio, his son: Beaumont;
Gonzago, Duke of Urbin: Lyly; Granuffo: Chapman; Don Zuccone,
a causelessly jealous lord: Jonson; Sir Amoroso: Decker; Herod
Frappatore: Marston; Nymphadoro: Fletcher.

This comedy was probably written in 1605, immediately after the
Fox and named the *Parasitaster* after Mosca, the parasite; but whilst
the one is a villain, Hercules is a noble character. The date is confirmed
by Dulcimel's remark, the picture of Hercules "speaks about forty,"
and again by Zuccone's jealousy, "this four year—ever since the old
Duke Pietro,"—evidently an allusion to the *Malcontent.* Gonzago is a
humourous satire on King James, and Herod's remark, "the duke is an
arrant doting ass," justifies the opinion, that in *Measure for Measure*
Lucio is a portrait of Marston, the man himself, and the Duke a complimentary portrait of James.

That an allegory is contained in the characters of the Princess Dulcimel and her attendant lady, Philocalia is incontestable—by the marriage
of Tiberio with Dulcimel Marston pays a flattering compliment to young

acceptance of the Roman general's protection, and his
beautiful address over the dead body, point to the

Beaumont as the son of Shakspere married to the comic muse ; whilst
in Hercules' admiration of Philocalia, *love of the Beautiful*, Marston
has given us a noble, grand, and truthful picture of the Shaksperian
muse in 1605 :—

Her. "Philocalia! What! that renowned lady, whose ample
report hath struck wonder into remotest strangers ? and yet her worth
above that wonder ? She, whose noble industries hath made her
breast rich in true glories and undying habilities?—she that whilst
other ladies spend the life of earth, Time, in reading their glass, their
jewels, and (the shame of poesie) lustful sonnets, gives her soul meditations—those meditations wings that cleave the air, fan bright celestial fires, whose true reflections makes her see herself and them ! she,
whose pity is ever above her envy, loving nothing less than insolent
prosperity, and pitying nothing more than virtue destitute of fortune.

Nym. There were a lady for Ferrara's duke! &c.

Her. I cannot tell—*my thoughts grow busy.*" Act iii., p. 51.

Marston, ever since his co-partnership with Jonson in *Sejanus*, had
been in disgrace, but Shakspere now hastened to acknowledge this
beautiful compliment by restoring him to favour in the very first lines
of *Lear* :—

Kent. "I thought, the king had more affected the duke of Albany,
than Cornwall.

Glo. It did always seem so to us : but now, in the division of the
kingdom, it appears not which of the dukes he values most."

From this time forth Marston remained faithful to his chief, painting
him as the noble Massinissa, the good Albano, and as Count Roberto :—

Isabella. " Here is a man of a most mild aspect,
   Temperate, effeminate, and worthy love ;
   One that with burning ardor hath pursued me.
   A donative he hath of every god ;
   Apollo gave him locks ; Jove his high front ;
   The god of eloquence his flowing speech ;
   The feminine deities strewed all their bounties
   And beauty on his face ; that eye was Juno's ;
   Those lips were hers that won the golden ball ;
   That virgin-blush, Diana's. Here they meet,
   As in a sacred synod."

      Insatiate Countess, Act i., sc. 1.

romantic Fletcher, Cæsar's Antony, Marston's friend
and pupil; and when Imogen rejoices in the loss of
the crown on the discovery of her brothers, 'tis Shakspere resigning the sceptre of poetry to Beaumont and
Fletcher :—" for the fate of these sons of Cymbeline no
source is known, it must have been Shakspere's own
ingenious invention."—*Gervinus*. For their enthronement, the two poets appear to have instantly returned
thanks in the *Honest Man's Fortune;*—Duke of Orleans:
Jonson; Earl of Amiens: Marston; Montague, the
Honest Man: Shakspere. The scenes in verse mostly
by Beaumont.

Sir Walter Ralegh was so affected by the death of
Prince Henry, that though he had, as he said, *hewn out*
the second and third parts of his *History of the World*,
he had not heart to finish them; that Shakspere was
also deeply affected by this event, we cannot doubt; and
it may with truth be said, in the grave of Prince Henry
lies buried the romantic drama, the musical soul of
Shakspere.

The Prince's death together with the marriage of the
Princess and her departure from the country may have
decided Shakspere on retiring thus suddenly altogether
from the stage. Considering the personal nature of
Cymbeline, and of Antony and Cleopatra, it becomes
probable Henry VIII. is also of a personal nature; that
Shakspere was seized with a sudden impulse of publicly
acknowledging his gratitude to those who had so
honoured him, "Eliza and our James," and in the
character of Katharine paying a tribute of affection
and esteem to the faithful partner of his life; whilst

in Cranmer and Gardiner we have the hid sense of Edgar and Edmund.

This feeling of gratitude and loyalty appears to have been the immediate origin of Henry VIII., Cranmer's speech being the key to the drama, the link that unites and gives a oneness to the whole: yet therein Shakspere acknowledges himself also *the subject* of Beaumont and Fletcher by the imitation of their freer and looser versification, adopted partly out of compliment to his friends, but with his usual judgment, the scenes referring to a period in the memory of persons still living. This opinion is confirmed by the prologue being an imitation of the prologue to the *Woman-hater*, from which the first line is taken, and the last line from the *Maid's Tragedy* :—

> *Amin*　　　　　　　　"I am forc'd,
> In answer of such noble tears as those,
> To weep upon my wedding day."
>
> Act i., scene 1.

It has been poetically imagined, the *Tempest* was the last of Shakspere's dramas, the mighty wizard addressing us in the words of Prospero :—

> "I'll break my staff,
> Bury it certain fathoms in the earth,
> And, deeper than did ever plummet sound,
> I'll drown my book;"

but not being troubled with poetic fancies, and having honestly, conscientiously, and with truth-seeking dispassion traced Shakspere through his dramatic career, I rest satisfied and content with the pleasing belief, that, though nearly thirty years are interposed, there is in the poet's heart a connecting link between the vision of Pericles and the vision of Katharine; between the dream of the youthful poet, and the dream of the Christian pilgrim.